STAR TREK 33:
THE KLINGON GAMBIT

A *STAR TREK*®
NOVEL

THE KLINGON
GAMBIT
ROBERT E. VARDEMAN

TITAN BOOKS
LONDON

***STAR TREK* 33: THE KLINGON GAMBIT**
ISBN 1 85286 282 3

Published by
Titan Books Ltd
58 St Giles High St
London WC2H 8LH

First Titan Edition March 1990
10 9 8 7 6 5 4 3 2 1

British edition by arrangement with Pocket Books, a division of
Simon & Schuster, Inc., Under Exclusive License from
Paramount Pictures Corporation, The Trademark Owner.

Printed and bound in Great Britain by Cox and Wyman Ltd,
Reading, Berkshire.

For Mike and Marilyn,
my favorite "Kring-ons"

THE KLINGON GAMBIT

Chapter One

Captain's Log: Stardate 4720.1

Mapping of the Class-Q type planet, Delta Canaris IV, continues. This planet, discovered three years into our five year mission, is providing a needed break from deep space routine for the crew. The violent gravity waves emanating from the planet require constant orbital corrections, but the added work might prove worthwhile due to the possibility of life on the planet. Sensor readings are positive although in a part of the life-spectrum indicating beings unlike any previously discovered by a Federation starship. Excitement among the crew runs high. Morale has never been better.

Captain James T. Kirk felt the deck of the *Enterprise* vanish from under his feet. Grabbing a handrail, he steadied himself until the gravity fluctuations had passed. He glanced around the bridge and saw his officers busy themselves countering the adverse influence of still another gravity wave from the planet below.

"Mr. Sulu, report," he ordered.

"Orbital corrections already made, sir," said the efficient helmsman. Sulu continued to punch in orders to the ship's control computer, his fingers almost a blur. Kirk nodded. The Asian knew his job and did it well. The captain continued his visual inspection of the bridge.

"Lt. Uhura, are those gravity waves affecting communications?"

"No, sir," she answered. "Subspace is clear all the way to Starbase Sixteen. Do you wish to transmit now?"

"Not immediately. I still have to finish the annual efficiency report."

"And if subspace transmission wasn't possible, you wouldn't have to do the report right away?" The Bantu woman's eyes sparkled.

"I didn't realize my motives were so transparent to the crew," said Kirk tiredly. "Those reports are due too often. I'd rather be with Mr. Spock, seeing what that planet down there really has to offer." He looked at the viewscreen and the dancing, shifting rainbow of the planet's methane atmosphere. "It looks just like Jupiter, even to the large red spot," he said, more to himself than to his communications officer.

"The similarity ends there, Captain," came the level voice of Mr. Spock. The Vulcan had come onto the bridge, and Kirk hadn't even noticed, being too engrossed in the sight of the gas giant. "Computer analysis of our previous sensor readings indicates life-forms similar to a sheet of paper."

"How's that, Mr. Spock?" Kirk looked at the imperturbable science officer, wondering if the Vulcan wasn't deliberately baiting him. He had noticed a sly sense of humor creeping into the Vulcan's words from time to time, but he had always discounted that as his own facile imagination at work. Humor wasn't logical and, above all else, Spock valued logic.

"This is a new life-form, probably sentient."

"Probably?"

"A ninety-four point two percent probability, Captain. The life-forms are slightly larger than your hand and less than a millimeter thick, due to the intense gravity of the planet. We have detected distinct roadways, structures believed to be cities and even indications of an ammonia ocean spanning trade."

"But they're only a millimeter thick?"

"Less than a millimeter. The exact thickness fluctuates due to food intake, movement and—"

"Thank you, Mr. Spock." Kirk sighed. "I would like to know more, but I am afraid I must leave it in your capable hands for the moment. The annual efficiency and promotion reports are due at Starbase all too soon. I'd be more than happy to have you file the reports except it is a captain's duty, and you are more efficiently employed studying Delta Canaris IV."

"Logical," agreed Spock, turning to his computer. His fingers inputted information as he stared into the blue dimness of his console display. Kirk knew the Vulcan was lost in a world of rapidly changing data, correlating it, digesting it and producing logical hypotheses for inclusion in the final report on the planet.

Reports, snorted Kirk to himself as he turned away. His life was plagued by a continual flood of reports. Status reports to Starfleet Command, matériel reports, utilization reports, efficiency reports—a starship captain had to be more of an accountant than a commander these days.

"Mr. Spock, you have the conn," he said, going to the turbo-elevator. The movement of the elevator didn't affect him like the fluctuations caused by the gravity waves from the planet. Long years in space had inured him to this familiar motion. The pneumatic hissing ceased, and the doors opened onto the deck containing his quarters. He had barely gotten to his desk when he remembered a disciplinary problem that he had failed to attend to earlier. Kirk punched the call button on the desk and said, "Mr. Scott to captain's quarters immediately. And bring your chief engineer with you."

He had just begun work on the reports when his door chime sounded.

"Come." Kirk straightened as he saw Scott and the engineering chief stiffly enter the room and stand at ramrod attention in front of him.

"Reporting as ordered, sir," said the dour Scots officer. "And I brought Chief McConel with me."

Kirk found it hard to look with displeasure on the chief. Very attractive, she kept her red hair pulled back from her forehead and held in a small knot at the side. He saw a perfect complexion marred only by a trace of grime on one cheek, piercing green eyes . . . and a mind that was as agile as her lithe body.

"Chief McConel, are you aware that gambling is not allowed aboard ship?"

"Aye, sir," she said, her slight burr a companion to Scott's.

"You're not denying that you were caught with elaborate gambling equipment in the engine room, are you?"

"No, sir, I am not."

Kirk sighed. "Chief—Heather—I don't care if there are games running. They keep the crew busy during slack times. You know that. This whole matter would never have reached my attention officially if you hadn't rigged the roulette wheel with that laser." Kirk leaned back, trying hard not to smile. "Tell me, how did you do it?"

"'Twas but a wee bit of hocus-pocus, sir," she said, brightening. "The roulette ball is painted black. A mite of a laser beam against the ball and it dances to whatever tune I choose."

"So that's how . . ." Kirk bit off his words. He had often wondered how he could have lost so much of his pay in such a short time at a casino on Argelius II. The captain shook himself back to the issue at hand, "Chief McConel, you will dismantle your gaming equipment—and that still you so cleverly hid in the machine shop—and put yourself on back-to-back shifts until I relieve you of the extra duty. Perhaps the added work will burn up that surplus energy of yours now being diverted to rigged games of chance."

"Aye, aye, sir."

"Dismissed. And Mr. Scott, a word with you in private." They both watched the chief leave, her behind twitching just the right amount as she went through the door. Scotty's heavy exhalation told Kirk more than words could have.

"She's quite pretty, isn't she, Scotty?"

"Aye, Captain, thot she is."

"And you let her get away with rigging the roulette wheel. It's you I should have on punishment duty, but I'm letting you both off this time. Nothing will be entered on her record. I don't want this showing up on the Enterprise's efficiency report. Those desk-skippers at Starfleet would jump all over something like this. I know you won't stop the gambling—you shouldn't—but don't let me hear any more about cheating. We will have fair contra-regulation gambling aboard this ship while I am captain. Do I make myself clear?"

"Pairfectly, sair!" The burr heightened in his words, and Kirk knew that Scotty wouldn't let his feelings for the chief get in the way of his duty again.

"Good. Now let's forget about those reports for a minute and have a little—"

The buzz of the ship's intercom interrupted him. He

stabbed down on the call button and said, "Kirk here."

"Captain, a message from Starfleet Command." Uhura sounded excited.

"Flash it on the screen, Lieutenant."

"I can't, sir," she said. "It's encoded and tagged. 'For Captain's Eyes Only.' You have to decode it yourself, sir."

Kirk felt momentary surprise at this. Highest priority messages were routinely squirted along in microbursts and received through devious computer-controlled equipment, making interception highly unlikely. To further encode a message was almost unheard of.

Almost.

"Send the coded message down by courier, Lieutenant," he ordered. Looking up at his engineering officer, he said, "Dismissed, Scotty. We'll have to have that drink later."

"Aye, sair. Be looking forward to it!" Smiling, the engineer left.

Kirk's attention focused on his tiny viewing screen, as soon as the security man delivered the message cassette. Row after row of numbers paraded out until the viewing area was filled. Leaning over, he opened the captain's safe, keyed only to his palm-print. The small decoding device inside hummed as he began copying the numbers displayed on the screen. When the message became intelligible, his face stiffened. Erasing the words, he activated the ship intercom.

"Bridge. Mr. Spock."

"Yes, Captain?" came the calm tones of his first officer.

"Lay in a course for Alnath II immediately. Warp factor eight."

"That is emergency speed, Captain."

"Aren't the engines up to it?" snapped Kirk.

"Of course they are, sir."

"Warp factor eight, Mr. Spock. Our presence is required at the start of another interstellar war." He sagged back in his seat for a moment, then hastened to get to his bridge. The *Enterprise* had to be made battle-ready before arrival.

"General quarters, general quarters. All stations, condition red. Repeat, condition red," intoned Sulu, his voice trembling slightly. He looked back over his shoulder at

Captain Kirk, sitting in the command seat, a mask of intense concentration freezing his features.

"But, Jim," protested Ship's Doctor Leonard McCoy, "they can't be serious about this. The Klingons wouldn't dare attack a Federation vessel. That's like ticklin' a bull with a feather!"

"Are you saying Starfleet Command ordered us here by mistake? No, Bones, that order was signed by Admiral Tackett himself."

The doctor hesitated, then said, "The Chief of Staff?"

"That's right. Unless the Federation Council had issued the order directly, it couldn't come from a higher source."

"What happened, Jim?" McCoy moved closer to insure more privacy. The bridge hardly seemed the place for this sort of confidential discussion, but he had to know.

"The Vulcan Science Ship *T'pau* has been destroyed. The instant the onboard computer ceased to register life readings, it automatically ejected the ship's recorder. All life aboard the *T'pau*, Bones, ended within a few seconds. No disease, no equipment malfunction, no collision in space, nothing was recorded to indicate what happened. Starfleet Command believes that recent activities by the Klingons in this region indicate high probability that they were responsible."

"A new weapon, Captain?" asked Spock.

Kirk only nodded glumly.

"But the *T'pau* wasn't armed!" exclaimed McCoy, beginning to show the intense emotions he kept checked until now. "They couldn't have resisted a Klingon warship."

"Mr. Spock, sensor readings." The Vulcan drifted back to his console and began studying the readouts.

"A dreadnought class Klingon vessel in orbit around Alnath II," he said. "There has been no indication they have detected us. We are still beyond their sensor's limits."

"They might be more heavily armed," conceded Kirk, "but our sensors are still better than theirs. A small edge, very small."

"Captain, I have located the *T'pau*. The ship is adrift and intact. No life readings from the vessel." Spock looked up, his face bathed in the harsh blue light from his computer readout screen. With his pointed ears, dark hair and sallow complexion, he looked like Satan himself. The only thing missing was the hint of cruelty.

Spock's face remained impassive as he read off the grim findings.

"Dammit, Spock," yelled McCoy. "Don't you feel anything for them? They were Vulcans!"

"Dr. McCoy," said Spock in his even voice, "I mourn for all tragic loss of life. The full information in this matter has yet to be determined." He turned back to his console, studying the sensor readings intently.

"Bones, quiet down," ordered Kirk, before McCoy could retort to Spock's reply. "I won't have you yelling at Spock like that on the bridge, especially not now while he is busy." He chewed on his thumb as he studied the viewscreen. The drifting *T'pau* appeared, no visible scar marring the small vessel's hull. "You get together a few of your personnel for a boarding party. I want a complete rundown of conditions aboard the *T'pau*."

"Right, Jim. And . . . sorry."

Kirk looked up at his medical officer and smiled slightly. He knew McCoy. The man was competent but sometimes let his emotions run rampant. McCoy left quickly, mumbling to himself, already selecting mentally the staff he would take.

"Mr. Spock, have Security beam over a team prior to medical examination. I want to make certain no booby traps have been laid for us. Mr. Chekov," Kirk said, addressing the navigator, "what of the Klingon ship?"

"Still in orbit about the planet, Captain," the young ensign responded briskly. "I have all phaser batteries fully charged. Awaiting orders!"

"Keep phasers at full charge—and keep your finger off the triggers until I give the command."

"Aye, aye, sir."

"Security team is aboard the *T'pau*," said Spock. "They report nothing unusual—except the corpses."

"Put it on the viewscreen, Lt. Uhura."

Kirk propped his chin on his palm as he studied the viewscreen. The sight aboard the *T'pau* made him shudder slightly. He could tolerate blood. A starship captain sees more than his share of combat and death. The eeriness of a ship emptied of life without visible struggle got to him. The security team moved swiftly through the corridors of the ship, relaying back the grim picture of Vulcans peacefully lying on their bunks, faces composed, hands folded across their chests, hinting at something wondrous by their expressions. All were dead. It was as if they had simply lain down and gone to sleep, dreaming pleasant dreams, never to waken again.

"Theories, Mr. Spock?" asked the captain. He could think of no reason for the demise of the *T'pau*'s crew. All the tiny details only a spaceman would notice were in perfect order.

"None, Captain. I must rely on Dr. McCoy's autopsies for further data."

"Beam over the medical crew," Kirk said into his intercom. He watched as the shimmering columns of energy solidified and the medical team, headed by McCoy and his chief assistant, Dr. M'Benga, dispersed through the ship.

"Lt. Uhura, any communication from the Klingon vessel?"

"None, sir. The ship remains in orbit. It doesn't seem to be following more than routine radio blackout procedure. I'm picking up radiation that wouldn't be present if they were operating under full battle conditions. Even assuming their deflector screens aren't as efficient as ours, they don't seem to be trying to avoid detection."

"Might I point out, Captain," said Chekov, "that there is no need for them to hide? That is a new Klingon dreadnought."

"I'm aware of that, Mr. Chekov. As I am aware that any battle with them will be one-sided. How far away are any of our own dreadnoughts, Mr. Spock?"

"The *Konkordium* and the *Dominion* are the nearest. Both are currently in dry dock at Starbase Seven."

"Starbase Seven?" Kirk felt cold all over. The dreadnoughts were in neither position nor condition to fight the Klingon vessel. Yet he would have to engage anyway, alone, with no support. The Klingons had violated the Organian Peace Treaty, using a secret weapon against a peaceful Vulcan scientific expedition. They must not be allowed to return to their own empire unscathed. A heavy cruiser might not best a dreadnought, but it was his duty to try.

The encoded orders from Starfleet Command had been explicit on that point: The *Enterprise* was expendable.

"Put me through to Dr. McCoy," he ordered Uhura. A hiss and McCoy's voice peevishly snapped at him.

"What do you want?"

"A report, Bones. What did it? What did the Klingons use to instantly kill a shipload of Vulcans?"

"Can't answer that. I'm beaming the bodies aboard, stacking most of them like cordwood into the cryogenic vaults until we can ship them back to Vulcan for burial. M'Benga will do the autopsies on the others, since he is more familiar with Vulcan physiology than I am. But we can't get the job done if you keep bothering us."

"Beam over a pair of the bodies and get back here yourself. Leave the other corpses in place and evacuate the vessel. Drain off the air; the hard vacuum of space will preserve the bodies as well as our cryovaults. I can't take the time for the transfer."

"But, Jim—"

"*Now*, Bones, do it now. Kirk out."

Kirk felt the eyes of his officers on him. Staring straight ahead at the viewscreen, his voice as calm as he could make it, he ordered, "Impulse power, helmsman. Take us to Alnath II, using the bulk of the planet to shield us from the Klingon vessel."

"Sneak attack, sir?" asked Chekov, both eager and apprehensive.

"It looks that way, Mr. Chekov. It looks as if that might be our only hope of success."

"I tell you, this is unlike anything I ever saw," said Dr. M'Benga, the body of the Vulcan partially dissected and spread before him on the autopsy table. "He is in perfect condition. There is no reason for this person to have died."

"None?" asked Kirk.

"I studied for four years on Vulcan to learn what I have, Captain Kirk. I never witnessed a death on Vulcan similar to this."

"Mr. Spock?" Kirk turned and looked at his science officer. Spock's eyes darted back and forth as he studied the numbers on the medical computer printout.

"I can draw no inference, Captain. Dr. M'Benga is best qualified to evaluate this data."

Kirk hardly believed his ears. Spock was as close to being nonplussed as he had ever seen him. The array of numbers meant nothing to Kirk, but the lack went further —it extended to his most highly trained officers.

"Radiation? Could it have been a radiation burst?" he pressed, hoping for some clue to the Klingon weapon.

"If so, it is no radiation we are familiar with," the doctor said. "The cells of the bodies are in perfect condition. No ionization indicative of gamma radiation or X rays. The central nervous system is in good shape, too. No contusions, lesions or evidence of struggle. Their deaths were most peaceful. When I go, I hope it is like that." The black doctor stared down at the corpse on the table.

"Thank you, Doctor. With any luck, none of us will be departing this vale of tears anytime soon.

"McCoy, Spock, a word with you." Kirk left M'Benga intent on the autopsy. When he had the officers aside, he asked, "Any indication of Klingon intervention?"

"None, Captain," said Spock. "I have fully analyzed the recordings made by the *T'pau*. At no time did any aboard even mention Klingon presence. Our own recordings taken after the crew's demise also lack positive indicators of Klingon action."

"McCoy? Did you see anything? A feeling, a tiny detail, anything?"

"Nothing definite, Jim. But the Klingons are warlike. We all know that. They would like nothing better than to destroy the *Enterprise* in battle. They live for war and the Organian Peace Treaty has robbed them of that for too many years."

"But the *T'pau*," protested Kirk. "Any sign the Klingons caused the Vulcans' deaths?"

"No, Jim, but they must have done it. They're in orbit around that planet, aren't they?" demanded McCoy.

"Yes, Doctor, the Klingons are there. And we must attack, it seems. Soon."

Command weighed heavily on James Kirk. He had studied the results obtained from the analysis of the Vulcan craft. Seventy-two dead, no survivors, no records as to the cause of the tragedy—and no evidence indicting the Klingons, either. That worried him the most. They were within the seven-hundred-and-fifty parsec treaty zone imposed by the Organians. The Klingons couldn't have attacked a Federation vessel without instant retaliation by the Organians—or could they?

The Organians were peaceful, alien, powerful, but they weren't infallible. They could make mistakes. If the new

Klingon weapon operated in such a fashion that it was indetectable by whatever means the Organians used, then the Klingon Empire would feel emboldened and attack with impunity. The United Federation of Planets couldn't run crying to the Organians. The Federation would have to deal with this threat. Swiftly. Decisively.

And Captain James T. Kirk was the instrument of that action. He had ordered strict battle silence. No communication with Starfleet Command was possible now. The slightest subspace squeak would alert the Klingons. The burden of decision was his and his alone. Admiral Tackett had entrusted him with complete discretion in this matter.

"Mr. Chekov, status."

"We are within forty planetary diameters of Alnath II," said the navigator. "All phaser banks are fully charged. Photon torpedoes are armed and locked in on horizon."

Kirk's eyes drifted back to the viewscreen. The planet loomed bright and shining, an M-class planet, another Earth with sweet spring rains and soft breezes and warming sunlight. The single point on the planet's horizon where the Klingon vessel would appear, if it maintained its computed orbit, appeared no different from any other point. At his command, that area of space would be filled with ravening phaser beams and a score of torpedoes, each one capable of destroying an entire planet's surface. So much power—and all his to command.

He felt the tension around him. It was palpable, a fist crushing him. Decision. All his. Attack the Klingon before the other craft could prepare for battle. Spock agreed this was the logical course of action. The Klingon ship was newer, more heavily armed, swifter. The *Enterprise*'s only advantage lay in surprise. If the Klingon warcraft could be damaged severely enough before their defenses stiffened, the *Enterprise* might survive the battle. Kirk wasn't even sure his ship could outrun the enemy.

Shaking his head, he tried to get rid of the ideas of "enemy" and "battle." The evidence failed to convict the Klingons. He didn't know if the Klingons had ever detected the Vulcan ship. Perhaps M'Benga and McCoy had missed some little-known virus. A plague of incredible virulence might have ravaged the crew, killing them quickly. But a wealth of data argued against this interpretation. Where would the plague come from? Not Alnath II. The planet had been cleared by Planetary Research as safe, as safe as any M-class planet could be. No diseases, no dangerous beasts, no hidden menace. But something had killed those aboard the *T'pau*.

"Deflector screens up," he ordered. "Prepare to attack as soon as the Klingon vessel clears the horizon."

"Four minutes, Captain," came Chekov's voice, quivering with ill-suppressed emotion. Kirk knew Chekov was like a racehorse in the starting gate. Nervous now, waiting, unsure of himself, but when the battle commenced, he would settle into cool, error-free activity.

"Captain!" cried Uhura, "I'm picking up a broadcast from the planet's surface. They claim to be part of the *T'pau*'s crew. No, they were part of the scientific expedition. They . . . it's so confused, sir!"

"Put it on the screen, Lieutenant. And you, Mr. Chekov, keep your finger off the phaser controls."

Reluctantly, the young ensign leaned back, his hands away from the deadly trigger button.

"Keep a close monitor on the Klingon ship's position, however," Kirk added. He looked to the viewscreen and saw the blue-tinted, craggy face of an Andorian staring back at him. One of the hearing stalks had been broken off in some past encounter, causing the alien to cock his head slightly toward his communicator unit.

"Who is this? Is that you, Captain Sullien? What is the meaning of abandoning us in this high-handed fashion? Answer me!"

"Mr. Spock, analyze and identify."

"The Andorian is a scientist of some renown, Dr. Threllvon-da, an archaeologist who has worked with other Vulcan expeditions. He appears distraught that Captain Sullien, the commander of the *T'pau*, has not performed in a manner meeting Threllvon-da's expectations."

"The transmission is real? It is not being faked by the Klingons?"

"Negative, Captain. It is real."

"Uhura, patch me through to the Andorian. And keep the transmission on as tight a beam as possible. I don't want any leakage warning the Klingons of our presence."

He heard buttons pushed, the communications computer being programmed to carry out his desires. A small hiss marked the opening of transmission to the surface of Alnath II.

"Dr. Threllvon-da? This is Captain Kirk of the Starship *Enterprise*. Are you in danger?"

"Danger?" squawked the Andorian. "Of course I am in danger. Always in danger of some upstart damaging part of the ruins. This is why I need my laboratory equipment aboard the *T'pau*. You get that scurrilous Vulcan back here with my equipment, or I shall lodge a very stiff protest with the Interstellar Studies Committee!"

Kirk thumbed off two-way communication and asked Spock, "Is he for real?"

"I am afraid so, Captain. Dr. Threllvon-da appears very upset at the loss of his equipment. The voice-stress analyzer has been set for the particular physiology of the Andorians, and the results show only annoyance at having his researches momentarily thwarted."

Kirk thumbed back the communication link. "Are you in personal danger from the Klingons, Doctor?"

"No, no, they are such a nasty folk, but they are no real problem. Always bothersome, but the delays I am forced to tolerate are even more bothersome. You up there, Kirk, I think you said your name was, get Captain Sullien here immediately!"

"I am afraid that's not quite so easy. The entire crew of the *T'pau* is dead. Perhaps you can shed some light on this."

"What? Dead? Of course not. We are all fine."

"Are there any Vulcans among your number?" asked Spock, standing near Kirk's right hand.

"No, none. All Andorians, of course. All scientists intent on studying these wondrous ruins. The artifacts alone will be worth a hundred fine research papers. Even that fool Thoron can successfully finish off his doctorate with the dissertation he can write now. Never thought he would amount to anything, but this discovery will benefit us all. It—"

"Doctor, please. Will you beam aboard the *Enterprise*?" Kirk glanced at Chekov, who pointed to the chronometer. The Klingon warship would cross the horizon in less than a minute. Even with the relatively insensitive sensor devices aboard the Klingon dreadnought, they could not fail to detect the *Enterprise*. Then battle would be joined, all advantage of surprise lost to Kirk.

"What? Leave? I suppose I can, for a short while. Without my equipment we are digging with our fingers.

Very unscientific. I do so need my ultrasonic brushes, too. One of those blocks can be destroyed with improper cleaning, you realize."

"One to beam up," Kirk said to the transporter chief. "Mr. Sulu, can you keep the mass of the planet between us and the Klingon, at least for a few more minutes?"

"Aye, aye, sir. We will have to achieve the same orbit as the Klingon, but that won't be any trouble as long as they don't try any quick maneuvering."

"Do so, Mr. Sulu." Kirk flipped his intercom switch again and asked, "Has the Andorian beamed up, Mr. Kyle?"

The transporter chief immediately answered. "Just arrived, sir."

Kirk heaved a sigh. "Now maybe we can find out what's going on around here." He glared at Spock as the Vulcan raised one eyebrow in skeptical response.

Chapter Two

Captain's Log: Stardate 4723.4

We continue to evade the Klingon warship until such time as blame can be attributed for the deaths of the Vulcans aboard the Science Ship *T'pau.* Before destruction of the crew, the *T'pau* landed a party of twenty-three Andorian scientists on the surface of Alnath II. The leader, Dr. Threllvon-da, is argumentative and not inclined to cooperate with our investigation. Further questioning will no doubt bring out valuable information.

Kirk and Spock went to greet the Andorian. The blue-tinted scientist paced nervously back and forth in the transporter room, his demeanor indicating extreme distaste for the delay.

"Dr. Threllvon-da, I am Captain Kirk. This is my first officer, Mr. Spock."

"A Vulcan," snorted the Andorian. "Are you people everywhere? Am I to be cursed by you till the day I die?"

"Cursed?" asked Mr. Spock. "That is illogical, a superstitious belief not in keeping with strict scientific principles. Might I suggest—"

"You may suggest nothing," snapped Threllvon-da, pulling himself up to his full meter and a half height. "You will get me the equipment I need to properly study those ruins, and you will do it instantly!"

"Uh, Doctor," said Kirk, trying not to further antagonize the Andorian, "there seems to be some slight problem. The *T'pau*'s entire crew is dead. Can you help us by giving some information?"

"Dead? They are dead? How unscientific of them. Is that what you were trying to tell me before in your confused manner?"

"Seventy-two Vulcans are dead, Doctor, tracelessly," said Spock.

"Humph, that explains why Sullien broke orbit," said Threllvon-da. "But that doesn't excuse his behavior!"

"Come, let's discuss this over refreshment," said Kirk, herding the Andorian toward the wardroom. "Mr. Spock and I are most interested in hearing all about your expedition's discoveries."

"Really? But of course you are. This will shatter all the preconceived notions of those upstarts back on Andor— and Vulcan, too!" Almost greedily, the white-haired Andorian rubbed his hands together.

"Come," repeated Kirk, ushering the Andorian into the wardroom, "be seated and let's get to know each other better. A scientist of your fame must have many observations to make about Alnath II."

"Such a pleasant world," said the scientist, barely noticing when Spock tapped in a recording command to the ship's computer. "I feel nothing but admiration for the survey team who discovered it and suggested that I should be the one to examine the find more closely. They knew the true value instantly and acted with amazing dispatch in calling me in."

"What discovery is this, Doctor?"

"The ruins! The ruins of a most advanced humanoid civilization. Such a puzzle, too. Only a single pyramid remains on the face of the planet to mark their passing. It is as if they eradicated all other indications of their existence to focus attention on that pyramid. Here, I have holograms taken of it."

Spock took the proffered plate and slid it into the computer on the table. It burbled hungrily, then focused the picture at the far end of the room. Kirk had to suck in his breath. Even though the picture was reduced in scale, he felt the overwhelming majesty of the pyramid. The ebon sides gleamed dully in the bright yellow sun, almost draining vitality from the light and re-emitting it in subtly altered form.

"How tall is the structure?" asked Spock.

"The scale is at the bottom," replied the scientist, lost in the three-dimensional picture of his discovery.

"That makes it taller than the *Enterprise!*" exclaimed Kirk. "You say the people of this planet built the pyramid. When?"

"You mean how long ago. Perhaps five thousand years B.P. Before Present," he added, almost as if lecturing a class of dullards. "At least that and possibly more like ten millennia. Perfectly machined to a few microns tolerance. And inside is a veritable museum of archaeological relics."

Spock allowed the computer to show the next holo. The interior seemed roomy, a single stone altar dominating the center of the chamber.

"What is the purpose of that?" asked Kirk, lost in the wonder of the discovery, in spite of himself.

"Don't know. Haven't had time to properly study it. Don't even know if it was an altar. Has all the markings of a pedestal for displaying something important, but I wasn't the first into the room, you know. Those Vulcans were."

"The Vulcans entered this room first?"

"Then they marched out, while I was still inspecting the base of the pyramid. They lined up and beamed back to their ship, leaving us all alone on the planet." The Andorian stood and moved through the hologram examining facets of the picture and chuckling to himself.

"Wait, Dr. Threllvon-da. The Vulcans left and you immediately went into the chamber?"

"No, no, not even then. These pictures were taken after we chased the Klingons away."

Kirk's face hardened. "Perhaps you will tell me exactly what happened on the planet. What Klingons?"

"Why, the Klingons who came after the Vulcans left. I was so busy setting up camp, I hardly noticed when they beamed down. They came with all that equipment of theirs. The minute I saw that they had such heavy machinery, I tried to put a stop to its use. Why, they might crush valuable artifacts under the treads."

"Let me get this clear," said Kirk, more confused than before. "The Vulcans entered the chamber, then beamed back without saying a word to you. Then the Klingons invaded, heavy equipment of an unknown nature being offloaded from their starship."

"I suppose that sums it up. The Klingons swarmed all over our camp, some of them getting into that chamber. But I convinced them to leave us alone. They are such nasty individuals, unpleasant, but amenable to persuasion."

"A Klingon who listens to reason rather than killing outright? This isn't like them. Mr. Spock, any comment?"

"Highly irregular, Captain. If the Klingons are responsible for the deaths aboard the *T'pau*, why should they allow unarmed scientists on the planet to live?"

"I can answer that. I told them I had already called Starbase Sixteen for aid. I hadn't, of course, since that puny communicator Sullien left hardly reaches into near orbit, much less through subspace. But the Klingons contented themselves with their own paltry pastimes after making an inspection tour of my camp."

"There is more of a mystery now than there was before," mused Kirk. "The Klingons have in orbit one of the most powerful vessels in this part of space."

"Yes, the *Terror* they called it. Such a quaint name," said Threllvon-da. "Puerile, also. It fits their activities, if I do say so. If they would redirect their energies toward scientific pursuit instead of building devices of mayhem, they would be better off."

"We all would, Doctor," said Kirk. Of Spock, he asked, "What do you make of this? A ship capable of destroying even the *Enterprise* and the Klingon commander leaves it in orbit for all to find. Do you think he even sighted the *T'pau?* Their detection equipment could have missed a ship that small."

"We can only assume that the putative weapon is of such a nature that it is not dependent on their sensors for its use."

"Weapon?" cried the Andorian. "What is all this about a weapon? I demand to be given my equipment. Find the *T'pau*—I don't care if they are all as dead as this bulkhead—and get me my tools. You are entrusted by the Federation, Kirk, to further scientific endeavors. This planet is the archaeological find of the century. I know it!"

"We shall see what we can do, Doctor," said Kirk, trying to keep his anger down. "Wait here while Spock and I tend to other matters. Come, Mr. Spock."

In the corridor, Kirk sagged back against the cold

metal of the bulkhead, thankful for the substantial support along his spine. He wiped off a bead of perspiration from his upper lip and shook his head.

"I don't know what to make of it, Spock. I'd say he was totally demented, except I've seen others act in the same manner."

"Total dedication to his work. A workable philosophy for a race with distinct tendencies toward aggression. This is a sublimation toward knowledge and away from war. Logical."

"I could use less of that so-called logical approach and more information." Kirk felt less in control of the situation than ever before. The Klingons had made no overtly warlike move against any Federation citizen, yet there was no obvious cause for the deaths of the Vulcans. The threat posed by the powerful Klingon warship hung like the Sword of Damocles over his head—and over the *Enterprise*, as well.

"There exists no reason to disbelieve Threllvon-da," observed Spock. "He is a scientist of some note, capable of concentrated activity directed to worthwhile ends, and his word is not to be questioned lightly."

"Should I question the Klingons, instead?" asked Kirk bitterly.

"Why not?"

Kirk looked at his first officer and said slowly, "You're right, Mr. Spock. Why shouldn't I ask them?"

"Lt. Uhura, open hailing frequencies to the Klingon ship."

"Captain!" Kirk couldn't pinpoint the person responsible for the outburst. He heard a half dozen voices mingling into one. Looking around the bridge, he saw surprise on many faces, outrage on others.

"You have your orders, Lieutenant. Carry them out. And Mr. Chekov, please remove your hand from the phaser controls. While I am speaking with the Klingon commander, I do not want any unfortunate nervous twitches creating an interstellar incident."

"Yes, sir," said Chekov sullenly.

"Is the channel open?"

"Ready, sir."

"This is Captain Kirk of the United Starship *Enterprise* sending greetings to our Klingon compatriots." Kirk heard a strangled gasp on the bridge and ignored it. "We have entered standard orbit around Alnath II and wish to pay our respects."

The viewscreen picture shattered as frequencies matched, then coalesced into the grim visage of a Klingon. The swarthy, saturnine face contorted into a sneer. The Klingon gestured to someone out of range of the viewscreen, then settled into his chair to glare at Kirk.

"Captain Kalan of the Empire Ship *Terror*. What do you want?"

"Blunt, to the point," murmured Spock. "Never qualify for the diplomatic corps."

"It seems that there has been some slight problem aboard the Vulcan Science Ship *T'pau*. Perhaps you could help us understand the problem more fully."

"No."

Kirk's eyes narrowed a little. "Are you refusing us aid? All aboard that ship are dead. This is violation of the terms of the Organian Peace Treaty."

"The Klingon Empire will never violate the treaty!" snapped the commander of the other vessel. "Weaklings in the Federation might, but never in the Empire's ranks will you find one such. What has happened to this so-called science ship?"

"Unknown. The *Terror* went into orbit immediately after the problem occurred aboard the *T'pau*. Did you detect anything unusual? Abnormal solar activity? Gravitational anomalies? Anything that might account for the deaths?"

"Captain Kirk, eh?" sneered Captain Kalan. "My information officer has finally supplied data on you and your starship. You realize that, in spite of your record, the *Terror* is the superior warcraft?"

"I hardly acknowledge that, Captain Kalan, in light of the recent modifications made to the *Enterprise*, but as you pointed out earlier, we come in the spirit of peace under the treaty. We desire only information and then we shall leave. What brings you to the Alnath system?"

"This space is open to both signatories of the Organian Peace Treaty," the Klingon said. "We explore. We . . . we seek knowledge just as those on the surface of the planet do. An archaeological expedition is currently studying the ruins."

"Indeed," came Spock's soft comment. "I have never known the Klingons to be interested in archaeological ventures. Their energies have been devoted totally to the waging of war."

"I know, Spock," answered Kirk. To the Klingon commander, he said, "The *Terror* seems heavily armed for the mere pursuit of knowledge."

"I will not bandy words with you, Kirk. Any attempt on your part to force us away from Alnath II and out of the system will be met with force."

"Are you threatening us, Kalan?"

Again the sneer, a white gash in the darkly complected face. "Of course not, Kirk. We will *defend* ourselves against all of our enemies striving to rout us from our rightful place in the heavens." The way Kalan said it left no doubt that there were few things in the universe he would have liked more than to use his "stern measures" against the *Enterprise*.

"The matching of a dreadnought against a heavy cruiser would be interesting," continued Kalan. "Our tacticians have often wondered if the superior mobility of the smaller craft could be efficacious against a more heavily armed and armored dreadnought. An interesting problem for our computers, eh?"

"If you say so, Captain. You may rest assured that no Federation citizen will attempt to prohibit you from your pursuit of . . . knowledge. Good digging."

Kirk watched Kalan's face contort into a mask of rage. The Klingon broke the connection before Kirk could. The nervous strain over, Kirk swiveled around to face his science officer.

"What do you make of that, Spock?"

"I am not sure, Captain. The Klingon appears eager for battle, but all Klingons are. If he truly thought his craft superior, he would attack without warning. That he hasn't indicates uncertainty."

McCoy came onto the bridge and sidled up beside Kirk's chair. "I heard part of the exchange, Jim. What Spock says is true. What's this, though, about our being refitted to stand up to a dreadnought?"

"A little bluff, Bones, nothing more."

"Bluff?" asked Spock, cocking his head to one side. "This is part of the odd game you call poker. Lying for the benefit of intangible gain hardly seems worthwhile."

"We couldn't expect you to understand, Spock. It's not logical," said McCoy. "And what you're doing isn't logical, either, Jim. Attack! Fire on the Klingons while we still have the advantage of surprise."

"The element of surprise is gone, Bones. And on what grounds can we justify such an attack?"

"The Organian Treaty! They can't deny us peaceful access to Alnath."

"They aren't," pointed out Kirk. "And they would like nothing more than for us to try to deny it to them. No, Bones, we are going to have to walk softly and see where the path takes us. There is more, much more, to this than meets the eye."

"I just hope that's not the garden path you're leading us down, Jim," McCoy said soberly.

Kirk flipped off the computer in disgust. He had gone over the Andorian's statement a hundred times, and still nothing significant came out of it. The scientist simply couldn't guess what had happened to the Vulcans, nor did he really want to spend time considering the issue. The transcript of the verbal exchange with the Klingon commander yielded even less information. Kirk had summoned up the most sophisticated programs lurking in the computer memory and still he had nothing concrete to show for the actions.

The Klingons lived in a suspicious culture, paranoid and warlike. The Klingon commander's behavior could be explained easily within those parameters. Nothing indicated responsibility for the Vulcan deaths, but Kirk could not find any tonal inflection, any gesture, any small detail to indicate the Klingons weren't responsible, either. He was certain that Kalan wished they had been; no love was lost between the Klingons and the Vulcans.

Kirk leaned back and closed his eyes, trying to relax. The strain of the past few hours caused his head to throb unmercifully. He settled his mind, allowing the image of a peaceful lake to form. He drifted downward into the warm water, floating, freed from gravity, no longer held prisoner by his own body. As the relaxing images worked in his mind, the dull pulsating ache slowly stilled and finally vanished. He opened his eyes to see Spock and McCoy standing in the opened doorway.

"Yes, gentlemen?" he said tiredly.

"Captain, the Klingons have begun to jam all subspace frequencies. We cannot contact Starfleet Command."

"It's about as I figured," Kirk said. "They aren't sure why we are here. They might not even be sure we're telling the truth about the *T'pau*. The Klingons have suspicious minds. Even if we showed them the bodies, they might think we murdered the Vulcans to have an excuse to attack them."

"Jim, you're saying that the Klingons aren't responsible for those horrible deaths!" blurted McCoy. "You can't have any proof of that!"

"I don't, Bones. I'm trying to look at all sides of this. What if—and I'm only saying what *if*—the Klingons are not responsible? Then we would be the aggressors if we attacked and the ones initiating an interstellar war."

"And if you let them get by with using a secret weapon capable of tracelessly killing, the entire Federation is endangered."

"True. I've got to decide. Soon. But which is it to be? Are the Klingons cold-blooded murderers or are they innocent bystanders?"

"Seldom have the Klingons been innocent bystanders, as you put it, Captain," said Spock. "Their jamming of our communications indicates some culpability on their part."

"Not necessarily, Spock. They don't know that we cannot summon up even one of our dreadnoughts. They don't know we're the heaviest armed starship in the region. It's simple protection on their part; they know they can pound us into atoms if the need arises. If we succeed in calling for aid, they don't know what might be breathing down their necks."

"This implies some guilt on their part. I say attack now!" McCoy slammed his fist down hard onto Kirk's tiny desk top. The captain looked up at his medical officer, eyes widening slightly. Seldom had he seen McCoy so distraught.

"Are you questioning a command decision?" Kirk asked quietly. "If so, you'd better make a good case."

"Indecision on your part is case enough," ranted McCoy. "A good captain commands. Make a decision!"

Kirk wished he could contact Starfleet Command and consult with others higher in rank. They weren't line commanders anymore, but they were strategists, tacticians, men and women responsible for far-reaching decisions. He wanted nothing more than to map and explore unknown worlds. The *Enterprise* wasn't a warship, not like the super-powerful dreadnoughts. Its mission consisted mainly of contacting alien cultures never reached by other explorers, of mapping and charting planets and even space itself, seeking life and peace—not war and death. A decision had to be made, and it appeared war resulted in either direction.

If the Klingons did have a secret weapon, they would continue using it unless stopped here. Even then, the respite was momentary. If the Klingon leaders felt the balance of power had shifted significantly in their direction, they would press their supposed advantage into full-scale warfare. On the other hand, if the Klingons were as they said, peaceful scientists exploring as the Andorians were doing, a sneak attack could start a new war. Opinion in unaligned worlds would be against the aggressor; Kirk cared little for his name living in history as the single man responsible for causing an interstellar war with the potential of killing entire planets filled with people. Trillions—more!—could die from a mistake on his part.

"Bones, I'm tired. My eyes burn from peering into the viewscreen, and my headache is returning. Give me something to relax me and let me sleep."

"But the Klingons . . . !" protested the doctor.

"The Klingons won't go away. Unfortunately. As long as this uneasy truce lasts, no one gets hurt."

"Shall I maintain general quarters, Captain?" asked Spock.

"Yes, do so. It might be a truce, but it is also an uneasy one, with neither side trusting the other. Inform me the instant the Klingons show any potentially dangerous movement. Now, please, let me rest."

Spock and McCoy left, but sleep didn't come easily for Kirk. He tossed on his small bunk, restless and tortured by the decision he would have to make. Even when sleep took him, he dreamed of flashing phasers and exploding photon torpedoes. It was not a good night for him.

Chapter Three

The war of nerves continues between the *Enterprise* and the Klingon vessel. Every change of orbit is countered by the other as we jockey for continual advantage. The tension mounts aboard the *Enterprise* and threatens to disrupt the efficient functioning of many departments. This breakdown in morale is unlike anything I have ever seen aboard a starship. Extensive searches of the ship's computer memory fail to reveal any other situation paralleling ours. I must act soon or serious breaches of regulations will begin to occur.

"Mr. Chekov, status report."

"*Terror* changes orbit to remain directly above the Andorian camp below. They keep their phasers trained on the scientists." The young ensign sounded bitter, resigned to inaction. Kirk sympathized with him, reading much of his own character into that of Chekov's. Kirk knew he hadn't been much different the first time he had been assigned to a starship. Puppy-dog eager for action, unmindful of the consequences, it took only a few bloody space battles to convince him fighting was only one of many methods for deciding an issue. Chekov would learn that, too, one day, if they all survived.

"Position the *Enterprise* in an orbit directly under that

of the *Terror*, Mr. Sulu. Use impulse power to maintain position as our orbit decays."

"Aye, aye, sir."

"Mr. Chekov, a word in private."

The ensign stood and glared at his commander, challenging him. Kirk heaved a deep breath and said, "I want to make a quick inspection of the ship, Mr. Chekov. If I leave the conn in your hands, do I have anything to worry about?"

The ensign brightened. "No, sir!"

"Good." Louder, for all on the bridge to hear, Kirk announced, "You have the conn, Mr. Chekov." He swung out of his seat and took the turbo-elevator down to medical level. Thoughts of a strange virus filtered through his vague uneasiness about the behavior of his crew. It seemed unlikely, but what had struck the *T'pau* might be working insidiously on the *Enterprise* at this very instant.

"McCoy," he said, entering the doctor's office, "have you time for a few words?"

"Naturally. I assume this is about the crew's unusual behavior. They're acting friskier than a colt on a sunny day."

"That's one way of putting it, Bones. Frisky." He snorted. "I am more inclined to say mutinous. Discipline is breaking down. I had to put Mr. Kyle on report for failure to be at his post. You know what he was doing? Sculpting. He was in the ceramics lab sculpting a small figurine."

"So?"

"So, Bones, Kyle had a spotless record. That wasn't like him. I asked why he had left his post while on duty, and all he could say was that he thought he might have a real career in the arts."

"Was he any good at the sculpting?"

"Come off it, Bones! That's not the question. Kyle is a good transporter chief, but his dereliction of duty could have imperiled lives. If we required an immediate evacuation of the Andorians on the planet below, Kyle would have been running his fingers through clay and not across the transporter control panel where they belonged. But a flawless record, top ratings, nothing but 'excellents' all across his efficiency reports and now this."

"Everyone has a momentary lapse, Jim. Don't be so

hard on him—or yourself. Take some time to relax and do what you want. Get away from all these machines." McCoy glanced around his office, almost overrun with flowering plants. "I find it restful to escape into here. Kyle probably got upset over the idea of breaking apart all those people, scrambling their atoms and then gluing them back together with that devil's machine of his."

"Some psychiatrist you are. You're actually defending his actions."

McCoy shrugged. "He's not letting the tension get to him like the others are. Some of the crew are beginning to fight. If they can't fight Klingons, they'll take it out on each other."

Kirk snorted, stood and began to pace in the tiny area provided in front of the desk. "That's another cut at me for not attacking the Klingons, isn't it? Well, Doctor, I am not going to do it. Not unless they make the first move."

"We'll all be radioactive dust if you let them shoot first, Jim."

"Listen, Bones, you mend the patients and I'll tend to running the ship."

"You're not doing a very good job, are you?"

Kirk started to retort angrily, then paused and got a firmer grip on his emotions. McCoy was right about that, at least in part. He was a starship captain and responsible for the crew of his ship. Whether he initiated the attack or not, he could not allow the morale aboard the *Enterprise* to sink lower. Kirk started to say something, thought better of it and left the doctor in his plant-filled office. Somehow, it was nicer getting out into the cramped corridors of the ship and away from the jungle of those green-tendriled plants.

"Spock," he called, stopping his science officer. "I'd like a word with you."

Spock stood impassively, waiting. Kirk envied his first officer his emotionless approach at times. While Spock could never know the joys of love or feeling, neither was he pressured by indecision. Everything reduced in his mind to its basic elements, studied in a straightforward manner, and then the most logical course of action was followed. Kirk recognized the problem with that approach; sometimes the most logical tack was also the most brutal. Less efficient, more humane choices could be made—on the basis of human feeling.

"I assume you are worried about incidents such as that?" Spock turned slightly and pointed with the tip of his chin toward two arguing crewmen. One took a round-house swing at the other, decking him.

Spock moved silently, his fingers finding the proper spot on the standing crewman's neck to apply the Vulcan nerve pinch. The man tensed and then sank to the deck, stunned.

"Get him back to his quarters," ordered Kirk. "But first, tell me what you were fighting over."

The frightened crewman stammered, "I-it was nothing, sir."

"Carry on." As soon as the men were out of earshot, Kirk added, "It's a sorry day when they're afraid of their own captain."

"My hearing is somewhat more acute than yours, Captain. Both men desired the same woman."

"*That* was the cause of the fight?" Kirk felt stunned. Incidents like that didn't happen aboard the *Enterprise*. He ran his ship carefully, never treading on the individual crewmen's personal lives, while keeping control over their baser instincts. It was a fine line and one Kirk strived to maintain. He saw all his work disintegrating around him with absurd fights.

"I'm sure it was, Captain. You must realize these men are highly trained and very aggressive. They like to fight."

"Mr. Spock, have the section heads meet in the wardroom in one hour. We've got some talking to do."

Kirk paced the corridors of the *Enterprise*, observing, noting, writing memos that would be delivered to the appropriate section heads at the meeting. In a way, Kirk felt good that the Klingon menace was at hand. This allowed him to put off doing his efficiency and promotion reports for a short while. By the time the Klingon problem was solved, one way or the other, he would either have time to whip his crew back into shape or it would never matter. To have to submit his reports now, though, would be a painful task. Crewmen wandered away from their duty posts to pursue hobbies, to lose themselves in drink, to seek solace in one another's arms.

He entered the wardroom to find his officers already

assembled. Spock began to call them to attention. Kirk waved such formality aside. He neither required it nor desired it. Preserving the integrity of his ship came first. Always.

"You are all observant people. You see ship morale vanishing. I find myself in the position of a peacetime garrison commander," he said, addressing the silent people seated at the horseshoe-shaped table. "Keeping peacetime armies honed to a fighting edge is difficult. With no visible enemy there is the distinct tendency to ignore discipline, to believe combat will never occur. This is human nature. It is also the way to disaster. Our situation is more complex, with the Klingons hovering so near. We cannot openly attack. This produces both sloth and inattention on the crew's part. They must think we will never need to go to battle. However, the *Enterprise*'s safety depends on constant vigilance. One brief instant of carelessness and we can all be dead. Do I make myself clear?"

"Yes, sir, you do," said Lt. Patten of Security, "but if we ride our divisions too hard, we might push them over the edge. If you know what I mean, sir."

"I do," said Kirk, nodding somberly. "Get them too keyed up and they will see ghosts. They will, in turn, fire on those ghosts, and the Klingons get what they want: war. It won't be easy, but it must be done: keep the crew at their posts, alert, but not so nervous they will make mistakes. That's all I have to say on the subject. How you accomplish this in your individual sections is entirely up to you. I will back your decisions. Now we'll have a few reports on the situation confronting us. Lt. Uhura."

The woman stood, a dreamy look on her face. "Uh, what, sir? I wasn't listening too closely."

"A report, Lieutenant." Kirk studied the woman, wondering what had gotten into her. Uhura was usually sharp, quick on the uptake, never at a loss for an answer.

"Oh, yes, the Klingons. They still have our communications blanketed. We've orbited six relay satellites to enable us to keep contact with the Andorian expedition, no matter where in orbit the *Enterprise* happens to be. I . . . I can't think of anything else, sir."

"What were you thinking about, Lieutenant? A few minutes ago."

Uhura looked at the table, a shy smile on her lips. "I was thinking about Dr. M'Benga. Isn't he handsome?"

Several around the table suppressed laughs. A cold stare from Kirk stilled them. "I see nothing funny in Lt. Uhura's reply. I asked her a question and I received an honest response. You all know your duties. Go about them. Dismissed."

Kirk watched his senior officers depart. A cold shiver raced up and down his spine. He felt control of his ship slipping from his grasp, and he didn't know why. He was a good captain, his finger always on the crew's pulse to detect unrest. The malady affecting both crew and officers seemed doubly serious when the Klingon ship was added to the equation.

It was an equation demanding immediate solution. Kirk hoped he could do it.

"I'll roast you over an open fire if you don't leave that alone!" the ship's nutrition officer shouted at Lt. Commander Scott. Scotty had pried loose part of the auto-chef control panel and scavenged inside for delicate electronic parts.

"Dinna get upset, mon," said the engineer. "This is whot I need for the engines."

"Hang your engines," the nutrition officer raged. "You'll starve us all. You took the serving control computer yesterday. I figured that might be all right if you really needed it to repair the engines, but I been asking around. You're stripping this whole damn ship and for nothing!"

"For nothing!" flared Scott. "How can you say that, mon? Those wee bairns will be as smooth as a baby's kiss when I tune them a'right!"

"I don't care about that. The crew won't eat that purple gruel coming out of the food processors. They blame me for it! Me, and I try to program the best meals possible. I can't do it when you rip out all the control electronics."

"Thair," said Scott with satisfaction. "I have whot I need." Smiling, he walked off, fiddling with the components. He hardly noticed others hastily slamming shut tool chests and flinging themselves across doors to prevent his entry. Few had escaped the engineer's depredations for parts for his precious engines. He swung into the engine room and held aloft his most recent prize.

"Ah, you have it," said Chief Heather McConel. "Now we can test our modifications. Put it right into the circuit. Ah, 'twas a fine day when the captain ordered me to this extra duty."

Love shone in Scott's eyes, both for the woman and for his engines. "Aye, thot it was. You always did have a way with the engines, but the extra duty paid off most handsomely!"

The intricate maze of wiring, computer assists and control panels ripped from a score of other locations filled space normally empty in the engine room. The pair of enthusiasts had driven the others in the Engineering Department away with their obsessive behavior. Kirk had assigned Chief McConel to work two of the three watches a day; she stood the back-to-back watches, caught a short nap and rushed back, hardly eating, to work on the improvements she and Scott had wrought in the matter-antimatter engines.

"No more positron leakage," she said with satisfaction. "Tightening up the force-field control worked, Mr. Scott."

"Aye, and a good idea it was, lass. You are a bonny mechanic!"

They tinkered further until McConel said, "A laser trigger is what we need. Otherwise, we must dismantle the main controls. I'm thinking the captain might not approve of that, with the Klingon birkie a'staring at us all the time."

"A laser trigger," mused Scott. "I dinna ken where one suitable might be found."

"I have an idea," the attractive chief said. "It might take a wee bit of thievery on my part, but in a good cause . . ." Her voice trailed off as she looked to the engineering officer for approval. She saw it in his eyes. Flashing him a bright smile, she wiped sweat from her dainty hands and was gone.

The others nearby had learned of Scott's foraging after their equipment. They weren't prepared to keep out Chief Heather McConel, too. And even if they had tried, her wiles would have melted the coldest of hearts. In less than an hour, she had convinced a technician in the metallurgy lab that he really didn't require the services of a low power laser, not for the time being.

Like a pack rat, she returned to the engine room and added her newest shiny trinket to the growing pile.

"Fighting again, eh?" asked McCoy, looking at the jagged wound on the crewman's arm. Every heartbeat caused fresh blood to well up red and thick. McCoy's thumb pressed harder into the artery to slow the loss of blood.

"It wasn't my fault, Doc," protested the crewman. "Three of them jumped me. I wasn't doing anything, just minding my own business, and out they came."

"Sure, that's the way it always is," said McCoy, using a pair of tweezers to pull out a shard of broken glass. He flipped down a magnifying lens and studied the wound to make sure he had gotten all the stray bits of debris. "Over a woman, wasn't it?"

The man jerked free of McCoy's grip, and the bleeding became more profuse. For a moment the crewman seemed confused. He couldn't decide whether it was better sitting and bleeding to death or having the wound properly cared for and putting up with McCoy's armchair psychiatry. Yielding to the sight of his own blood leaking out, he thrust himself back into the firm hands of the surgeon.

"Yeah, Doc, it was. I mean it wasn't anything, really. She and I hit it off all of a sudden, and then I found out she not only had a husband but two other boyfriends. All three of them ganged up on me."

"Couldn't you work out some more amicable solution between the, uh, the five of you?" McCoy held to old-fashioned ideas. The various pairings and couplings aboard the *Enterprise* often amazed him, sometimes amused him and always made him feel that he was out of step, a century too advanced for his true roots.

"Hey, watch it; you're hurting me," the man protested.

"Sorry," said McCoy insincerely. He pulled the arm closer and called to Nurse Chapel. "Get the anabolic protoplaser, please." Gone was all thought of the crewman's personal failings. He now became the perfect surgeon operating on a minor wound. His hand reached out, and Nurse Chapel smartly slapped the protoplaser into his grip. "This won't hurt a bit," he said, pulling the crewman's arm up into the light so he could watch the protoplaser neatly close the wound and begin to heal the sundered flesh.

A tiny buzz marked the triggering of the protoplaser. As McCoy applied it to the man's arm, a blue spark arced out and burned the patch of skin directly under the blunted snout of the instrument. Again, the man jerked free of McCoy's grasp.

"What are you, Doc, some sort of quack? That hurts like hell."

"Gimme that arm!" said McCoy, irrationally savage. "The damned thing didn't work. Machines! They never work when you need them. Nurse! Number six needle. Gut. I'm going to close him up properly . . . none of this depending on machinery."

"Dr. McCoy, is that wise? The protoplaser just malfunctioned. I can get another one from stores."

"I'm the doctor, Nurse Chapel, and I asked for needle and thread for a suture. Are you going to get it for me or do I have to get it myself?"

"Look, Doc, if you're too busy . . ." began the crewman.

"Lie back and shut up. The machines aboard this ship are all falling apart. I knew it. I always knew they would one of these days and I was right. But you're in good hands. Few doctors in the fleet today could rely on the old tried and true methods."

"Here, Doctor," said Nurse Chapel, handing him the needle and gut for the suture. "Do you want me to get him a bullet to bite down on or will you just use a shot of redeye?"

McCoy glanced up at the nurse, then paused, thinking. "Local anesthetic, one cc endorphin-stimulator." The efficient nurse whacked the desired pain-killer into his palm. He jammed the injector into the side of the crewman's throat, then tossed the emptied injector aside. "Surprised it worked. Might have to go back to hypodermic needles."

"Don't sound so excited about it, Doc," said the crewman. "I get nervous thinking about pointy things after what they did to me."

McCoy touched one ragged piece of flesh with the tip of the needle; the man didn't flinch. "Endorphin's surging. Only thing left is to get this fixed up." Quickly, expertly, he began suturing the wound. The crewman winced at the sight of the needle going through his pain-deadened skin, but the ordeal was short lived. McCoy looked down at his handiwork and smiled.

"That's more like it. Don't depend on the machines. They'll give out on you when you least expect it."

"Don't wish too hard out loud, Doc," pleaded the crewman. "I'm a mechanic on the life-support systems. If they go down and the backup doesn't work, we'll all be breathing garbage—or vacuum." The man looked uncomfortably at the discarded protoplaser, back at the needle held triumphantly in McCoy's hand, and then fled.

"He should be happy an old-fashioned, country-style doctor like me was here. M'Benga would have panicked if he found a protoplaser that didn't work."

"Doubtful, Dr. McCoy," said Nurse Chapel. "M'Benga's training was most thorough on Vulcan."

"Bah, Vulcan. They're the worst of the lot, always depending on computers and electronic gadgets to think for them. Strip them of their playthings and they wouldn't know what to do. Give me the simple life. Like it used to be."

McCoy went off to his plant-overrun office—still talking to himself—and plopped heavily into his pneumatic chair. The faint hissing as the device altered shape to match his contours irritated him. But the chair was comfortable, he had to admit. In the isolation of his office, he began to think that he had made the wrong decision. His wife's leaving had precipitated his entry into Starfleet. They'd needed doctors, and he had needed to escape from Georgia and all the unpleasant memories around the hospital, his house, the entire planet. But running away hadn't erased the memories. He knew now he could travel ten thousand light-years and still be right where he started— trapped in the maze of his own memories.

McCoy slipped off to sleep, one thought going over and over in his mind: It is better to have loved and lost than never to have loved at all.

"Any further information from the tapes of the *T'pau*, Mr. Spock?" asked Kirk.

"No, sir, nothing. I have Lt. Avitts studying them now for a different perspective."

"But you don't feel you missed anything?" goaded Kirk, smiling slightly.

"I don't *think* I missed anything, Captain," replied Spock haughtily. "I desired another interpretation of the data to see if it matched my analysis. Also, this is good training for Lt. Avitts."

"How is she working out, Mr. Spock? She came highly recommended from Starbase Seven."

"She is weak in physics, although her chemical and biological knowledge is adequate. More training will alleviate the lack."

"Very well, Mr. Spock. Carry on." Kirk turned his attention back to his own problems. Spock continued to run computer simulations of possible causes of the *T'pau* disaster, not finding anything with higher than a point zero three probability. As the last of his programs ran to completion, Spock straightened and asked, "Permission to leave the bridge, sir."

"Granted, Mr. Spock. But be back in an hour to relieve me."

"Aye, aye, sir."

Spock walked briskly from the turbo-elevator toward Lt. Avitts' quarters, his mind constantly turning over the problems confronting the *Enterprise*, studying them from various points of view. He chimed at the door, heard the woman's clear voice say "Come" and walked forward, the door opening smoothly in front of him.

The Vulcan glanced around the room, taking in all the details with that one sweeping survey. Lt. Candra Avitts sat at her tiny desk, now strewn with reports and survey tapes. Her desk computer squealed at the forced input of information, straining to analyze the data. The wall decorations were decidedly feminine, some being flat photos of various holovid stars while others were of a more scientific nature. The faint scent of jasmine in the air matched the woman perfectly. Spock wondered if she had analyzed her own pheromones to find which perfume would complement her natural odors. He hardly thought chance could have produced such a satisfying end result.

While appreciating but unmoved by feminine charms, that being the logical course of action in light of his seven year *pon farr* cycle, the human part of Spock tacitly approved of Lt. Avitts.

"Lieutenant," he said in his brusque, businesslike manner, "are you finished with the report on the *T'pau?*"

"Here it is, Mr. Spock," she said, pushing the computer cassette across her desk to the science officer. "I checked the data, thought about it, and have drawn a blank. I can't figure out the cause of the *T'pau* disaster, either. There is only one thing, but . . ."

Spock said nothing. His eyebrow raised in interrogation.

"Well," she said reluctantly, "I had the idea that the

Vulcans might have been participating in some religious observance, meditating perhaps, and somehow lost track of their bodies."

"An interesting speculation," said Spock. "While it is logical that a Vulcan would desire to attain an existence freed of material body and achieve one of pure intellect, it hardly appears possible that all the Vulcans aboard the *T'pau* could achieve such a state simultaneously."

"You're right, Mr. Spock," the woman said, lowering her gaze as if she had done something wrong. "But then, you always are."

"I act from the precepts of formal logic. While logic cannot always produce a correct answer, it succeeds more often than it fails. Therefore, it is logical to employ logic all the time. The odds are decidedly in your favor."

A long silence fell, then Lt. Avitts looked up, her eyes dewy. Spock stared into her hazel eyes, unable to fathom the woman's racing thoughts. She nervously shuffled the tapes on her desk and stood, moving away with a lithe movement reminiscent of a hunting jungle cat.

"I . . . I've been going over the data transmitted up from the planet by Dr. Threllvon-da," she finally said. "It's interesting."

"Please brief me on this data. I have not had time to study it fully."

"Oh," Candra Avitts said. "Well, sit down, Mr. Spock. Make yourself comfortable."

He seated himself in the small chair pulled out from her desk while she dropped to the surface of the bed, crossing her long, slender legs under her. She began to gesture, pointing occasionally at the computer readout screen.

"The data are fascinating, Mr. Spock. The Andorian has dated the pyramid at more than three million years. Evidence indicates it was used until approximately fifty thousand years ago. After that, no record exists of what happened to the planet's inhabitants. Threllvon-da believes they all migrated to another world, though for what reason he cannot as yet say."

"Illogical. The sun of this world is stable, and geological records indicate no sign of past adverse solar activity. No blight could reduce the ranks of a truly advance culture." Spock cocked his head to one side and peered at the lieutenant. "Any ruins discovered other than this single pyramid?"

"No, Mr. Spock," she said, straightening her legs again and moving perceptibly closer to the Vulcan. "This is the only artificial structure on the planet. The satellite mapping confirms it. Threllvon-da believes the inhabitants lived in underground cities. Look, that's part of his report." Candra Avitts reached out, a delicate hand resting on Spock's shoulder as she pointed out the pertinent portions of the Andorian archaeologist's report.

"Fascinating," Spock said, turning back to the woman.

"And so are you," she said, her voice hardly a whisper. "Is . . . is it true you feel no sexual urges except every seven years?"

"That is essentially correct, except for certain special instances. Vulcans are, above all else, logical. Sex is illogical."

"It can be interesting," the woman said, her hands running down the front of Spock's uniform tunic. "But what you say applies to pure Vulcans. You have a human side. I know. That's what attracts me to you."

A raised eyebrow was her sole answer.

She kissed Spock. He neither resisted nor responded. Hotly, she clutched his muscular body and pulled it toward her, attempting to get him fully beside her on the bed. A slight movement freed him from the circle of her arms.

"Lieutenant, your conduct is most unbecoming to an officer. It is also illogical."

"Logic can't provide all the answers; you said so yourself. Relax, Spock, relax—with me! Nature intended for us to enjoy ourselves, our bodies. Otherwise, we wouldn't be able to feel pleasure."

"This pleasure, as you term it, can be derived from the solution of a complex problem. It is not dependent on physical gratification."

"So you *do* feel pleasure," she exulted. "I thought so. The slight smile that dances on your lips when you have finished a complex computation, the sparkle in your eyes as you do your duty well, those are all clues that you feel pleasure. You have kept the human side of your nature bottled up inside. Release it! With me!"

She attempted to pull his lips back down to hers. Spock broke her grip and said stiffly, "Lt. Avitts, I expect the report on the archaeological finds to be readied by the end of this watch."

He left her sitting on her bed, tears forming at the corners of her eyes. But, as the door silently closed behind him, Spock held out his hands. They shook in an uncharacteristic fashion. The emotional ocean heaving inside him was even more unusual. Spock hastened down the corridor, hoping no one noticed his lapse.

Kirk swiveled back and forth in his command chair, making certain every station of the bridge ran smoothly. The viewscreen held a fixed image of Alnath II, with an inset picture of the Klingon ship orbiting a few hundred kilometers above the *Enterprise*. To remain in the same relative position between Klingon and archaeological site required the use of impulse power at computed times. Lt. Sulu attended to that while Ensign Chekov drilled the phaser crews.

Kirk worried his lower lip as he studied the back of Chekov's head. The young officer was so much like he had been just a few years ago. Impulsive, inclined to accept surface impressions instead of reasoning through situations. Yet, the potential for a good starship commander was there. Kirk hoped that they would all survive this encounter with the Klingons and give Pavel Chekov his chance one day.

He heard the doors of the turbo-elevator, but didn't turn to see who had come onto the bridge. Since his watch neared an end, he decided the most likely candidate was Spock. Kirk wasn't disappointed in his little deduction. He heard the Vulcan's voice ring out.

"Lt. Uhura, have you succeeded in penetrating the communications blanket established by the Klingons?"

"No, Mr. Spock. I've been busy trying to maintain contact with the expedition on the planet."

"Why can't you attempt both? Surely this is not beyond your capabilities as communications officer. You have tremendous resources at your command. Might I suggest you employ them to better ends?"

"Mr. Spock!" cried Uhura, outraged. "I'm doing the best I can. To maintain even a laser com link with the planet is difficult. I've had to hook a computer into the laser head to—"

"Excuses are for incompetents," he said, anger tinting his voice.

"Mr. Spock," said Kirk hastily. "A word with you."

"As soon as I check my station, Captain."

"Now, Mr. Spock," Kirk said, the knife-edge of command in his voice.

"What is it?"

Kirk blinked twice to believe he actually had his first officer in front of him. The petulant manner was totally unlike the Vulcan. It actually showed stark emotion on Spock's part.

"Your attitude leaves something to be desired, Mr. Spock. Is anything wrong?"

"Nothing, Captain," replied Spock, his voice calming. Kirk scowled as he watched the transformation back into the Spock he knew. But the change didn't halt. Spock metamorphosed into something colder, as if in response to the emotional outburst.

"You seem distraught."

"That is a human failing. I have purged all such from my mind. Uncontrolled emotions create physiological disorders and are generally unproductive in a thinking, rational being."

"Yes, that's right, Spock. I was just . . . testing you. As you were."

"Thank you, sir." Spock pivoted and marched to his station, more robot than flesh and blood. Kirk had barely turned his attention back to the Klingon ship on the screen when he heard Uhura arguing with Scott.

"No, I won't allow it, Mr. Scott. You can't have it!"

"But just a wee one, Uhura. Ye won't miss it, I assure ye!"

"What's going on?" demanded Kirk, fed up with the bickering he had noticed all around him. "Scotty, what do you think you're doing under the communications control panel?"

"The engines, sair. The chief and I have a wee project under way. To tune the engines. We figure we canna maintain this orbit without more power. Fifteen percent more power can be diverted to the impulse engines with our modification."

"Mr. Scott, you have reduced the crew to eating a putrid-looking gruel. . . ."

"But it tastes good and is good for us, sair!" protested Scott.

"Stripping the autochef, however, was not a good idea. Mr. Kyle, when he deigns to report for duty, claims you have disabled three of the transporter units by pulling out the crystal oscillators, and Chief McConel cleverly talked one of the metallurgy technicians out of a laser being used to run tests on hull samples from the *T'pau*."

"But, Captain, thot's not as important as this! The engines!"

"Mr. Scott, the engines are in fine shape. They always are, thanks to your diligent efforts in that respect. But you are carrying this too far. You've become obsessed with modifying them to achieve even greater . . ." Kirk cut off his comment in mid-sentence. Breathing deeply, exhaling, trying to calm himself, he continued. "Mr. Scott, desist. Do not dismantle one, I say again, *one* more item of non–Engineering Department equipment for use in the engines unless I specifically authorize it. Do I make myself clear?"

"Aye, Captain, but this bonny triac from Uhura's panel will . . ."

"Mr. Scott!"

"Aye, sair. I ken what yer a'sayin'."

Kirk felt drained. Spock fluctuating emotionally before his eyes, Scotty and his pilfering, Chekov and his wild desire to blast the Klingon out of space, the crew becoming edgier and edgier—all took their toll on his nerves. He felt like more of a mediator in civil disputes than the captain of a starship. The dull throbbing in his head refused to die down as long as he sat in the command chair.

"Mr. Spock, you have the conn."

For the first time, Kirk added under his breath, "And I hope the ship survives it."

Chapter Four

Captain's Log: Stardate 4731.0

The Klingons continue to jam subspace transmission. I have ordered Lt. Uhura to prepare a message capsule to be launched to Starbase Sixteen in case of attack. Morale continues to deteriorate due to the strain of the Klingon presence. Fighting between crew members is commonplace, and standard disciplinary techniques do not work. I grow more concerned about the inability of the crew of the *Enterprise* to effectively react should the need arise.

"Mr. Spock, come with me."

Spock glanced up from his computer console and nodded curtly. His nimble fingers worked over the controls, and the computer whispered to a halt, the fast flow of data ceasing. Like a robot, the science officer stiffly walked to stand in front of his captain.

Kirk sighed and turned to Chekov, saying, "You have the conn, Mr. Chekov. Spock and I will be on a Captain's Tour of the ship. Notify me if there is any change in the Klingon orbit."

"Aye, aye, sir," the ensign said. Kirk started to change his mind and leave control of the starship in Scotty's hands. That meant prying the engineer away from his beloved engine room. Chekov might not be the best choice for command at the moment, not with the way he fondled the firing triggers so lovingly. One light brush across those sensitive contacts would send out prodigious lances of phaser fire capable of starting another interstellar war.

He sighed again, more heavily. No, let Chekov retain the conn. Scott would only begin subverting the entire ship's mission to eking out another fraction of a percent efficiency from the engines. Chekov at least kept a close watch on the Klingons.

Kirk entered the turbo-elevator, Spock at his side. The doors slid shut and Kirk said, "We're pretty much at a standstill as far as the Klingons go, Mr. Spock. I want to get that damned efficiency report out of the way."

"Is it necessary, Captain?"

"It gives me something to do. I realize that if the Klingons destroy us it's worthless, but it might give me a clue to reversing the trend in the crew's decaying morale. You have noticed?" He studied his science officer. Spock stared straight ahead at a blank wall as if hypnotized.

"I have, Captain."

"Comments?"

"You humans operate on a set of tenets that are totally illogical. I find no rational way of explaining your actions, even at the best of times."

"I didn't think so." The doors opened and Kirk strode out onto the life-support control deck. The normally bustling activity had been quieted to a few crewmen wandering in a daze. Kirk simply stood and stared as one officer staggered by, obviously drunk.

"Lt. Gordon, explain!" snapped Kirk.

He watched the young man's eyes unblur, but sobriety was fleeting. Propping himself against a bulkhead, the officer slurred out, "Howdy, Cap'n. Howcum you're down here slumming?"

"Stand at attention, Lieutenant," said Spock, his voice sharp and cold.

"Sure, if you say so. Been drinkin' just a bit. And why not?"

"What section are you assigned to?" asked Kirk, trying to remember. Seeing that he wasn't likely to get a coherent answer from the man, he turned to his tricorder and requested data from the ship's main computer. He went cold inside when he saw the answer flash across the tiny screen.

"Lt. Gordon, not only are you supposed to be on duty,

but you are charged with maintaining the life-support systems computer."

"Huh? Yeah, I guess so."

"Take us to your duty station."

The youth stumbled off as Kirk and Spock followed silently. The door to the life-support computer room slid open. Lt. Gordon dropped into his console chair and smiled.

"See? Nothing's wrong. Never is."

"Mr. Spock. Correct this mess immediately."

The Vulcan leaned over and began altering the readings displayed on the computer readouts.

"Whatsamatter? Don't mess around with that!"

"Mr. Gordon, you have allowed the carbon dioxide level to rise precipitously aboard the *Enterprise*," said Mr. Spock in his robotic voice. "If it had risen another few percentage points, the crew's functioning abilities would have been grossly impaired."

Kirk punched the wall communicator and barked, "Security. I want Lt. Gordon relieved of duty until further notice."

Security arrived and Kirk left, his fists shaking impotently. In the hallway outside the computer room he said, "Spock, I've never hit a junior officer but I came close then. He actually endangered the ship. I'm going to courtmartial him all the way back to Starbase One!"

"That is your prerogative, Captain. The regulations are most exact on this subject. Dereliction of duty in any circumstance is intolerable. In a condition-red status, it might be fatal to all."

Kirk stopped and considered how Spock reacted. No hint of emotion. No attempt at presenting a balancing side. The old Spock he knew would have pointed out the irrationality of human beings, how strain made them crack at times. Not now.

"Let's check the engineering deck, Mr. Spock. The efficiency report needs a bright spot right about now. Mr. Scott has never disappointed me with that aspect of his behavior."

They rode the turbo-elevator to engineering deck, but Kirk felt the cold lump forming in his stomach even as they reached the engine room. The crew members fought openly, not even attempting to stop as he and Spock walked among them. He didn't try to break up the fights;

he felt too cast adrift. This couldn't be the *Enterprise* he had worked so hard at honing to a fighting edge. This wasn't his crew. His crew snapped to attention in the presence of a senior officer, they did their jobs quietly and to the best of their abilities, and most of all they *cared*. He failed to understand what these people—he no longer thought of them as a crew—cared about. Like Kyle, like Gordon, like all the others, they seemed intent only on their own personal pursuits. Fighting, wenching, drinking, they were disreputable and not fit to wear the Federation uniform.

"Mr. Scott, Captain," announced Spock in his computerlike voice. Kirk wanted to strike out, to rage, to shake sense into the Vulcan, but he restrained himself. Only a carefully thought-out plan would bring Spock out of his absolutely logical phase and back to being the best science officer in the fleet.

Kirk looked around the engineering room and shook his head. Many of the control panels had been scavenged. Cables ran from them to a device in the center of the immense room. The device hummed with a power so immense Kirk failed to understand it. All he saw were the superconducting cables running from the electrodes at the ends of the matter-antimatter engine nodules.

"Mr. Scott, explain this!" snapped Kirk.

"Aye, Captain," said Scotty, smiling from ear to ear. "'Tis a bonny construction. The chief and I put it together. Sets up a feedback loop to increase the warp engine power by twenty-two percent."

"Twenty-three percent, Mr. Scott," said the red-haired Chief Heather McConel. "'Tis a good thing you puttin' me on the extra duty, Captain Kirk. Otherwise, we'd never have done it by now."

"Is the integrity of the ship compromised?" Kirk asked, his eyes confused by the loops of heavy power cable running into the device. No matter how he gazed at it, he felt twisted around inside as if it threatened to pull him into an energy vortex.

"Cap'n, would I do such a thing?" cried Scott, outraged.

"No, Mr. Scott. Just you and the chief . . . never mind. Carry on."

"Aye, Cap'n, that we will!"

He shook his head and quickly left. In the hallway he dodged male and female crew members chasing one another. Their intent was obvious by their state of undress:

"Saturnalian rites, Captain," Spock said calmly.

"Let's go to the sick bay, Mr. Spock. I want words with Dr. McCoy. Perhaps he can explain what's happening to my ship."

They took a gangway up one deck and came to McCoy's office. Kirk knocked and walked into the fern and leaf overrun room. He pushed some of the clinging vines out of his path and found McCoy sitting disconsolately at his desk, staring at a blank bulkhead.

"Bones? Are you all right?" he asked anxiously.

"Hmm? Oh, yes, Jim. I'm fine. Just . . . thinking." McCoy reluctantly pushed away the dreams fluttering across the edges of his mind. "What can I do for you? Some plastic surgery on Mr. Spock's ears?"

"That is most offensive, Doctor," said Spock.

"Offensive? How can a being who denies emotions find anything offensive? Answer me that, Spock."

"Doctor, you have no call to . . ." Spock suddenly turned and stalked off. Kirk watched in surprise as his first officer left. He felt more and more confused about the situation aboard ship and told McCoy this.

McCoy leaned back in his chair and hoisted his feet to the desk. "I guess it's a reaction to being surrounded so long by the metal walls, Jim. The folks aboard the *Enterprise* hunger to get back to their roots. They want to feel the dirt under their feet, see the sun rising gold and hot on their faces, run through the meadows after a spring rain. They're going stir crazy locked up in the bowels of this mechanical monster."

"Don't call my ship a monster, Doctor," said Kirk. He took a deep breath and tried to relax. He mustn't get involved in a verbal battle with McCoy, he told himself. He had to work out his problem—soon. The fate of not only the *Enterprise* but the entire Federation depended on it.

"It *is*, Jim. It's unnatural. All those machines. We're their slaves, you know. We tend them and they give us back what *they* choose. Let the crew get out on a farm and watch their attitudes change for the better. No more fighting, no more wanton sex. Try it and see what happens, Jim."

"You can take the man out of the country, but you can't take the country out of the man," quoted Kirk. "But I think you may have an idea, Bones. We've been in space for a long time, and the crew hasn't had a decent shore leave since Argelius. The mapping mission, now this. Yes, maybe you're right."

"Of course I am! Let's find a spot to settle down and use the hull plates as plowshares. You'll see that—"

"I wasn't considering colonization, Bones. And no one will use the hull of this ship as scrap, not even Scotty if he thought it would increase the power of his engines."

"What?"

"Never mind. I like the idea of some shore leave. Within limits, down on the planet's surface, with full scanner contact to make certain the Klingons don't attempt anything."

"The Andorians seem to be doing just fine."

Kirk laughed, the sound short and staccato, devoid of real humor. "I think Threllvon-da would do fine on any planet with a ruined civilization to dig up. He couldn't care less about our problem with the Klingons. He wants to make his archaeological discoveries more than anything else in the universe."

"See, Jim, he's getting back to the soil. He wants the dirt to run between his fingers. He feels an affinity with nature."

"He'd burn off an entire populated planet to make the ruins, if the idea ever occurred to him," said Kirk. "I want the . . ."

He was interrupted by the sound of a bitter argument outside the doctor's office. Kirk rose lithely and went to the door. He opened the panel and clearly heard the voices of Nurse Chapel and Lt. Avitts.

"You slut! You just want to take him away from me!"

"He loves me, you second-rate pill peddler. And no one steals him. He's his own man and he's chosen *me*. Spock is mine!"

Kirk closed the door and slumped back into the chair in front of McCoy's desk. "Doctor," he said, "make up the first shore leave party roster for me—on the basis of maximum deviation from recorded psychological norm. Let's get rid of the worst at the start. Maybe that'll cure some of the contagious insanity we seem to have caught."

"First party to beam down, sir," came Lt. Kyle's dreamy voice. Kirk walked over and stood behind the transporter chief, his eyes studying the settings on the transporter controls. He didn't quite trust the chief since he had found him sculpting what the man called "a modern day Venus di Milo" with three arms.

"Beam them down to the planet's surface, Mr. Kyle," he commanded, watching the flicker of the telltales. All went smoothly. The six in the transporter shimmered and turned to insubstantial pillars of pure energy. With tiny pops, they vanished from the ship to be reconstructed three hundred fifty kilometers below.

"Next party ready," said one of the security men, leading in another group. Before Kirk gave the command that would send them after the first group, the wall intercom buzzed and demanded his presence.

"Kirk here. What is it?"

"The Klingon commander is charging us with violation of the Organian Peace Treaty, Captain," came Mr. Spock's unemotional voice. Kirk wondered at the change in his science officer. He seemed back in the totally emotionless phase, a one-hundred-eighty-degree switch from when he had stormed from McCoy's office.

"I'll be right up, Mr. Spock. Keep Captain Kalan pacified the best you can till I arrive."

The swarthy face of the Klingon commander filled the viewscreen. Kirk gingerly lowered himself into the command seat and stared at the Klingon for a few seconds, then pressed the button on the seat's arm that completed the audio circuit with the *Terror*.

"Greetings, Commander Kalan."

"Don't attempt to bandy words, Kirk. I knew you would violate the treaty at the first opportunity."

"Explain yourself, Captain. Your words are being recorded and will be transmitted to Starbase Sixteen."

"We are jamming your communications. Nothing will be sent out, murderous swine! You send armed teams to the planet's surface to conquer my peaceful scientists."

"Captain," said Spock quietly, "his men are armed with the latest Klingon sidearms. Many have weapons vastly more powerful than our ray guns. All our ground parties are armed only with Type I hand phasers."

"I know, Mr. Spock. Thank you." Louder, to the Klingon commander, Kirk said, "I believe you have misinterpreted our motives. None of our crew has attacked. There have been no confrontations."

"Because I have not allowed you time to amass sufficient forces on the planet!"

"Captain Kalan, might I point out that you already possess numerical superiority over Federation forces on the
surface of Alnath II? I am landing only a scientific support team to aid Dr. Threllvon-da in his explorations. His
credentials speak for themselves. He is most peaceful."

"Is the Vulcan in charge of this so-called scientific support team?"

Kirk saw the trap forming and cleverly avoided it.
"Captain, would I send Mr. Spock on such a trivial mission? His abilities are better utilized aboard the Enterprise. No, I have ordered his assistant to the planet.
Spock, get Lt. Avitts here on the double."

"A trick. You keep the Vulcan in reserve. He is a master tactician. You will move him to the planet when you
are ready to attack."

"Attack, Captain? Hardly," scoffed Kirk. "I meant it
when I said this was only a peaceful support team. Ah,
Lt. Avitts. I have placed you in charge of the landing
party. What is your principal duty aboard the Enterprise?"

"Assistant science officer, under Mr. Spock," she said,
glancing at the Vulcan and flashing him a winning smile.
Spock never moved a muscle in response.

"She lies. She is ordered to tell these falsehoods."

"Captain Kirk," said Candra Avitts hotly, "I do not lie.
I consider this the finest assignment possible in all of Starfleet Command. Mr. Spock is a marvelous instructor and
the Enterprise is the top ship in the mapping of newly discovered worlds. It is a great opportunity for me."

"Pah. But send her down. We watch you carefully,
Kirk, and one single indication of hostility will spell the
end for that rusty space tug of yours. The Terror will
blow the Enterprise to atoms!" The Klingon commander's
finger stabbed down at an invisible button, and the screen
powered down.

Kirk leaned back and breathed heavily. "That was
some verbal battle," he said. "Comments, Mr. Spock?"

"None, Captain. The Klingon is most perturbed about
added crew beaming down to the planet. Their mysterious
activities must be threatened by too many Federation personnel nearby."

"Lt. Uhura, have the comsats been able to pick up any intelligence on the Klingon movements on the planet?"

"No, sir," answered Uhura slowly. "The satellites pass over the archaeological site only once every three hours. Our sensors inside the comsat have so far failed to penetrate their jamming blanket."

"They are growing more sophisticated in their electronics," mused Kirk. "Remind me to look into that, Mr. Spock." He spun in his seat to face the dark-haired Lt. Avitts. He gazed into her hazel eyes and wondered at her involvement with Spock.

There was no doubt she felt strongly about the Vulcan, but what did Spock feel for her? Kirk had no easy answer. Under normal circumstances, he would have laughed any possible involvement off as space gas. Not now. Not with Spock swinging from starkly logical to overly emotional. He couldn't get those tears out of his mind. Spock had cried in frustration and anger.

"Captain?" asked the assistant science officer. "Is it all right if Spock joins me? I'm hardly the one to command such a—"

"You are in command, Lieutenant. And if you ever want to gain experience you'll simply do the best you can —without Spock." He watched her reaction, then continued. "I don't want Spock on the surface—yet. The Klingon would take that as a strategic move against his ground forces. While Spock is a first-rate science officer, the Klingons tend to think of him as a military tactician. We dare not stir them up until we can get to the bottom of this mystery."

"And then, sir?"

"Then we'll continue to play it by ear, Lieutenant, just as we're doing now. Get your gear together. I want you to aid Threllvon-da in whatever manner possible. Try not to antagonize him too much. And report back periodically on the movement and activity of the Klingons. I'm interested in discovering what they're doing with that heavy equipment on the surface."

"Aye, aye, sir," the lieutenant said, straightening.

"Dismissed." He spun in his seat and watched her go. To Spock, he said, "A pretty woman, isn't she, Spock?"

"I hardly concern myself with such human appraisals, Captain."

"Of course not, Spock. Carry on."

Spock returned to his computer console, but Kirk didn't fail to see the slight tremors shaking the Vulcan's hand.

No, Mr. Spock, he thought to himself, you don't concern yourself with purely human things like love, do you?

"I don't know what else to do about it, Bones," said Kirk to the doctor. He leaned back and stared off into the space behind McCoy's head. The cabin walls crushed in on him and made him think McCoy might be right about claustrophobia caused by too many years inside the ship.

But that had never bothered him before. He knew no other environment but starships. Neither did most of his crew, space-trained all. The problems of the deaths of the Vulcans, the Klingon menace and the lost civilization on the planet below had added too much strain to an already overtaxed crew. That had to be the trouble.

"You did the right thing, Jim. Want another drink?" The doctor held up a cut crystal decanter filled with smoky liquid.

"That stuff's potent. Get it from Chief McConel's still?"

"Private stock. Seems our 'Chief of Distilling' has broken down the still and isn't producing her fine vintage stock any more. She and Scotty are too engrossed in fine-tuning the engines."

"Heather McConel's given up on the still?" Kirk hardly believed it. "She turned out the finest impulse engine fuel in the sector. Who's taken over the business?"

"I haven't checked lately. Perhaps no one, though I suspect the purple slop coming out of the autochef might make good mash. It's certainly sour enough."

"Hasn't that been fixed yet?"

"You haven't been down to the wardroom lately, have you, Jim? I prescribe a *double* dose of medicine for you." The doctor poured the liquor into a tumbler and passed it over to the captain. "Seems like everything on board's gone to hell in a hand basket. Can't explain it except everyone's gotten their fill of being buried in the metal maw of this beast."

"You're talking about my ship, Bones. Watch it," Kirk warned tiredly. His words were almost knee-jerk responses. The fiery liquor burned all the way down to his stomach where it pooled and allowed warmth to spread throughout his body. Slowly, almost reluctantly, he relaxed.

"Everyone's looking out for his own selfish interests," mused McCoy. "Never seen a thing like it before. Nowhere in Starfleet has anything like this happened. It's just that I *feel* like I can do anything I want. The power's at my fingertips, just waiting to be used. I have to try and use it."

"For what, Bones?" asked Kirk. He stirred uncomfortably in the chair, aware that McCoy had touched the very thing gnawing away inside him. He felt the power, too, whatever that power might be. But he didn't seek out a simpler way of life freed of machines as McCoy did. All he needed to be happy was a resolution of the morale problem aboard the *Enterprise*—and to be free of the Klingon vessel hanging a few thousand kilometers above in orbit.

"For what? For whatever I think's the most important. I want to feel a patient healing because *I* did something right, not some damned machine. What do I know of the innards of an anabolic protoplaser? It's just some gadget handed to me. I'm trained to use it, but what does it really do? There's nothing to compare with the feeling of actually stitching up a wound and knowing I did a good job."

"So you broke the protoplaser," sighed Kirk. "I heard about that, Bones. That crewman got very upset with you for using monofilament wire to lace him up."

"It was gut and he should be glad. And I didn't break the damned protoplaser. It did that all on its own. Let Scotty fiddle with it. I'll depend on these." McCoy held up his hands in front of his face and stared at them. "In the old days, a surgeon's skill depended on the steadiness and sureness of his hands. No more. Some damned machine can be programmed to do just about everything. I stand and watch. No involvement in the surgery, to speak of. That's not the way it ought to be."

"The computer-driven autosurgeon doesn't make mistakes."

"And it can't be brilliant, either. A human can. That's what all this unrest among the crew's about, Jim. They want a bigger share in their own destiny. Fewer machines and more humanity. Mark my words, that's what they're up over."

"I can't buy it, Bones. Why now? The strain? That's incredible. They've been under worse pressure and not gone space happy. It's as if the worst—or the best—of their desires are being given free rein. They can't control themselves anymore."

McCoy laughed and drained his glass, filling it to the brim once more before he spoke. "Look at the cat fights Lt. Avitts and Nurse Chapel get into over Spock," he said. "Unrequited love and yet they act like it's the most important thing in the universe."

"Is it really unrequited, Bones? Have you seen the way Spock has been acting? He's like a flip-flop switch, going from totally unemotional to hysterical."

"Hysterical? Spock? You're exaggerating, Jim, but I did get the feeling there's more emotion lurking in Spock than he wants to let out. Hysterical," McCoy said again, a smile curling up at the corners of his mouth. "I'd like to see that with my own eyes."

"No, you wouldn't," Kirk said. "It's the same as watching a valued friend slowly self-destruct. It's tearing him apart, just as surely as the other crewmen are being torn apart. They have unreconciled desires inside and can't handle them anymore."

"Is the ship in danger?"

"More so than it's ever been—and I don't think the Klingons are the worst of it. They're not going away, but this internal disintegration bothers me the most."

"Drink up. The doctor prescribes another stiff jolt of this forty megawatt joy-juice. Try not to worry about it so much, Jim. Let the crew have some of their leave down on the planet and morale will improve. Mark my words."

"I have Lt. Avitts down on the surface now," said Kirk, "along with a scientific team to help Threllvon-da. Whatever it is affecting my crew, it's not from the planet below. I've run psychological profiles on Threllvon-da while he was aboard the ship and matched them with ones from our computer records. They match almost exactly. He and the others in his party are as normal now as they were five years ago when the profiles were put into the computer memory."

"Normal," said McCoy slowly. "What's normal? Living with machines all around? Not natural, just not natural. The old ways were best. Let's go start a farm down there, Jim. Looks to be good farmland. A few hectares under cultivation's all we'd need for the first year or so. Then we could expand once we needed more."

"You're a doctor and I'm a starship captain," said Kirk sharply. "I sincerely doubt you have any desire to root around in the dirt scrabbling out a ground gripper's subsistence living."

"No, I guess not," agreed McCoy, "but it sure sounds like a nice way to live."

"You're as space happy as the others," said Kirk, eyeing the doctor over the rim of his glass. He took another sip of the liquor and put the glass down, resolving not to drink any more. He couldn't afford to have his wits blurred, not now.

"All of us are different from the way we were," said McCoy. "But that's progress. I wonder if Klingons have the same problems aboard the *Terror*."

Kirk frowned, then said slowly, "I wonder if they do. I just wonder. . . ."

Chapter Five

Captain's Log: Stardate 4732.9

The Klingons play a game of waiting. The morale
abroad the *Enterprise* continues to deteriorate. Crew
members are more intent on their own selfish interests than in the greater good. I fear someone will be
inattentive to duty and create the incident the Klingons desire. Waiting is too wearing. We must initiate
action.

Uhura leaned back in her seat at the communications
console, her mind roving light-years away. How nice it
would be to have Dr. M'Benga actually notice her. She
sighed. The man was so handsome. Why did he have to
be totally engrossed in his medical researches? The constant probings into the bloodstreams of all members of the
Enterprise seemed to produce so little in the way of
knowledge. She knew she could teach him much more
pleasurable things—if only he would examine her more
closely.

She had other, more productive—and enjoyable—pursuits planned for them when lights flashed across the width
of her communications console. The woman blinked and
glanced down, her mind slipping back into its normal efficient operation. Analyzing, coming to the proper conclusion, she punched down several buttons. The computer
gurgled contentedly, absorbing the flow of information
from the broadcast.

"Captain Kirk!" she called out. "Transmission from the Klingon vessel."

"For us?"

"Negative, sir. They're using a microburst pulsing on a tight subspace beam. I'm intercepting through one of the comsats."

"A good thing we put them in orbit," said Kirk. "Decipher the Klingon message as soon as possible, Lieutenant. I am most interested in the content."

Kirk slumped in his command seat and turned back to face the viewscreen. The scene changed slowly as Alnath II rotated beneath them. The view from this height made him weary and heartworn. He longed to be on the surface of the planet, the wind rustling through his hair. He pushed the bucolic thoughts from his mind. He'd been listening to Dr. McCoy too much. Let the doctor harken back to Earthly scenes. James T. Kirk was a starship commander. Man belonged in space. He was living proof of that. His dedication and involvement with new planets, mapping and the contact of alien civilizations barely understandable by human standards proved that. Nothing was more exciting or challenging, nothing. He belonged among the stars, not at the bottom of a gravity well a planet deep.

"The computer is working, sir," came Uhura's clear voice. "The coding is the most complex ever used by the Klingons. It is a variant of an earlier, less complicated one."

"Yes, yes, Lieutenant," he said impatiently. He hated to press for details. Uhura was at least doing her job. He shouldn't anger her for being too involved in it. A quick glance around the control deck showed that Uhura, Spock and Chekov were the only ones minding their controls. Sulu wandered around, joking and laughing with the others, more intent on socializing than on maintaining the ship's heading.

"Captain," said Spock, "the computer analysis of the beam quality is finished, also. Do you wish the technical parameters of the transmission?"

"Later, Spock. I want to know what Captain Kalan considered so important that he had to punch it through our jamming."

"The message reads," started Uhura, " 'Harken, High Lord Admiral Kolloden, from Kalan, commander of the dreadnought *Terror!*'" Kirk chafed and shifted impatiently in his seat, crossing his legs, uncrossing them and then leaning forward to hear the meat of the message. "'Equipment functions at eighty percent optimal efficiency on the surface of Alnath II. Results within three planetary rotations.'"

Uhura looked up at Kirk. "This next part is confusing, Captain. I'm not sure if the computer translated it properly."

"Let me be the judge of that, Uhura. Hurry, out with it"

"Aye, aye, sir. The communication continues: 'Disciplinary action has been instituted against members of the crew, pursuant to Standing Order One. All twelve of the mutineers have been charged, tried and found guilty. Executions occurred at dawn equivalent, Zero Base Time. The left hands of the mutineers have been preserved; the remainder of their corpses have been dishonored and fed into the plasma torch.'"

"Mr. Spock, verify," ordered Kirk. He frowned while his science officer translated the Klingon transmission as a check on Uhura's accuracy.

"Lt. Uhura's decoding is essentially correct, Captain. The Klingons further note the mutineers' names. One of them was Kalan's own daughter."

"There's no chance that they wanted us to intercept the message?" Kirk pressed. "I know the Klingon electronics isn't as sophisticated as ours. They must know it, too. Are you sure that they didn't intend for us to read that message?"

"Unknown, Captain. It is of extremely low probability that the message content would be as it is if they intended for us to intercept. Why should Kalan suffer personal shame if it wasn't a true report?"

"A good point, Spock." Kirk leaned back in his seat, his chin resting on his fist. He thought hard about the message Uhura had tapped. Kalan had disciplinary problems aboard his ship even more extreme than those on the *Enterprise.* While the Klingon familial ties weren't as strong as those on most Federation worlds, they were potent. Offspring were groomed to shed nothing but glory on the parents. If Kalan had actually executed his daughter for mutiny, the Klingon commander had been faced with

a dilemma exceeding anything Kirk had dealt with so far.
So far.

"Mr. Spock, any indication as to the cause of the mutiny? Is the message complete enough to extrapolate details?"

"Conjecture only, Captain," came the imperturbable voice. He might as well have been discussing the price of flame lilies on Altair VI. His inflectionless speech had begun to grate on Kirk's nerves. And in that lay the seeds of discontent. Mutiny, perhaps. Kirk had to analyze his own feelings and try to understand the frustrations he felt.

"Let's have them, Spock."

"The planet below is emanating some type of force undetectable by our—or Klingon—instruments. This force causes extreme unrest among both crews precipitating the altercations we have been witnessing."

"That's not a complete explanation, Spock. The Andorians have not been affected, not visibly. They are happy and healthy and content to dig away at their ruins. Also, no sign of fighting appeared aboard the *T'pau*. Explanation?"

"None, Captain. I find the idea of a selective force implausible."

"Selective? You mean a force that only accentuates aggression in certain people?"

"Perhaps people with a predilection in that direction. But this still leaves unexplained the deaths of the Vulcans and certain atypical behavior not linked to aggressive tendencies."

"What behavior is that, Spock?" Kirk asked, turning in his seat to study his first officer. The Vulcan stiffened perceptibly and shook slightly as if fighting a major emotional battle inside. No sign of that fierce conflict reached his face.

"Behavior such as exhibited by Dr. McCoy. He has become pathological in his distrust of machines. He refuses to allow the computer to perform routine laboratory tests. The doctor insists all such tests be done by his assistants in a manner reminiscent of the twentieth century. Most primitive, to say the least." Spock scoffed.

"Other examples?"

"Commander Scott is obsessed with his engines to the point of ignoring other duties."

"And what about yourself, Mr. Spock? Any unnatural urges on your part?"

"I remain in full control of myself, Captain." The shaking of his hands ceased, and he covered himself again with a veneer of impenetrable calm. He had fought down his raging emotions and become a robot, a perfect thinking, moving, emotionless Vulcan machine.

"I see," said Kirk. "Do you notice any changes in me?"

"That is not for me to say," replied Spock.

"No, I suppose not. Very well, Mr. Spock. Please examine all facets of the data. Analyze your computer and instrument readings. Take into full account the information Lt. Uhura has garnered from the intercepted Klingon message and report your findings to me. I want to know the most probable cause of this . . . unrest. I will not tolerate its acting adversely on the crew of the *Enterprise*."

"Aye, aye, sir." Spock turned back to his computer and began punching in the information. Kirk rose and left the bridge, deep in thought.

Kirk dozed, his dreams troubled. The nightmare figures darted like insubstantial ghosts, haunting him and drawing him into actions he feared. He fought to maintain a mental equilibrium, to attain the perfect compromise between the dual aspects of his own nature. He couldn't be the soldier and race off to battle. The enemy ranks swelled even as he gazed over them. His fear grew. He had to retreat and consider other methods of winning. Defeat went against his nature, but attack was out of the question.

No aggression. Only a settlement with the phantoms of his dreams gave peace. He argued and shouted, cajoled and harangued—and was winning the dream-battle when his door chime pulled him harshly back to reality.

"Um, who is it?" he called out, rubbing the sleep from his eyes. His head still spun from the rapid transition from shifting dream to the substance of the *Enterprise* around him.

"Spock, sir. Request permission to enter."

"Come."

The Vulcan marched into the cramped quarters and stood at attention.

"What is it, Spock?"

"Sorry to disturb your sleep, but I find that the data at hand are not adequate for me to reach a statistically significant conclusion. I request permission to beam down to Alnath II and personally study the planetary surface, the fields interacting there and the nature of the archaeological site discovered by Threllvon-da."

"Can't you get all that from up here? I don't want to risk you down on the surface, not with the Klingons itching for an excuse to start firing at us."

"I believe the groundwork has been properly laid for my investigation, Captain. Kalan might object to my presence on the planet, but he will not attempt to use that as the reason for breaking the Organian Peace Treaty. Probability is point nine eight that he will do nothing but verbally protest."

"Is your investigation at a standstill otherwise?"

"It is, Captain. Data collected by others lack the immediacy needed for full interpretation. You realize how important that aspect of any experiment is."

"Yes, Spock, I do." Kirk's mind threw off the gauzy blanket of sleep and began to race. The need to push ahead gnawed at his insides. This stalemate didn't suit him, yet he dare not overtly act. Sending Spock to the surface to observe Threllvon-da and collect further information concerning the source of the theorized force field disrupting discipline seemed made to order. It wasn't a violent act, yet was a positive one and one which tossed Kalan onto the horns of a dilemma. The Klingon had to worry about Kirk's motives in sending Spock while tending to the unrest aboard the *Terror*.

"Do I have your permission to beam down, sir?"

"More than that, Spock. Take as many technicians with you as you think you'll require."

"None will be necessary, Captain. Lt. Avitts is already on planet."

Kirk looked sharply at his first officer. He tried to detect any of the telltale emotions he had witnessed before. The obvious attraction of the lieutenant for Spock might provide a reason for Spock's desire to beam down. But Kirk found no trace of anything but stark duty in the Vulcan's features.

"You may leave when you are ready, Mr. Spock."

"Thank you, Captain. I have my tricorder and can beam down immediately."

"Take care that the controls of the transporter are properly set," Kirk said suddenly. "I wouldn't want my first officer's atoms scattered between here and Vega."

"Do not worry. All will be in perfect order." Spock turned and left, the door hissing shut behind him. Kirk laid back on his bunk and tried to sleep, but his mind had become too embroiled in the "what ifs" of the situation. All he could do was hope for the best.

The transporter beam split Spock into a billion component parts, shuffled those parts around and then reassembled him on the planetary surface. The coarse gravel underfoot caused him to stumble slightly. He hesitated until his muscles adapted to the slight difference in gravity field and then strode off toward the dig.

The excavations were unimpressive, but the rising pyramid gleamed black and ominous in the sunlight. In spite of himself, Spock stopped and simply stared at the imposing structure. The perfection of that pyramid impressed him greatly. The black sides were so highly polished they had become mirrors.

"Spock!" came the joyous cry from his right. He turned and saw Candra Avitts running toward him.

A lump formed in his throat. She was so stunningly beautiful. Her long hair drifted back from her face, caught and held by the strong wind blowing across the gravel plain. He took a step toward the woman, stopped, swallowed and brought his wild emotions under stern control.

It was un-Vulcan to feel the emotions he felt except during *pon farr*. He took a deep breath, settled his mind and presented only the stoic exterior to Lt. Avitts when she came to a halt beside him.

"Oh, Spock, I'm so glad you're here. Why didn't you tell me you were beaming down? I could have prepared a proper reception for you."

"No reception is necessary. I am here only to observe Threllvon-da's techniques and to take readings of the fields peculiar to this planetary mass."

He glanced down at his tricorder and frowned slightly. He felt vexation at missing an important datum. He hadn't been paying attention to his primary duty because of the arousing nearness of his assistant. He fought and won another internal battle over his emotions.

"What's wrong, Mr. Spock?"

"Unknown," he said, studying the readouts of his tricorder. "This is a most unusual reading." He watched the indicator race off scale, then slowly return. Over and over the tricorder repeated this process until it settled down into a normal reading for a class-M planet. "Most odd. My tricorder has malfunctioned."

"Oh, no, Spock," Lt. Avitts said brightly, her eyes full of love for him. "That happened to my tricorder, too. It went wild for a few minutes before adjusting."

"Adjusting to what, Lieutenant?"

"I don't know. But mine works fine now. Come and see the excavations around the pyramid. Dr. Threllvon-da is doing wonders!"

She grabbed his arm impulsively and pulled him toward the excavation site. All the way to the pit Spock continued to study his tricorder. The readings bounced up and down but finally settled into an acceptable range as he and Avitts neared the pyramid. Spock had no chance to pursue the tricorder information due to Threllvon-da's sudden appearance.

"You there, Spock, isn't it? Yes, Spock. Where is my equipment? I demand to know! We are digging with our bare hands. I need the equipment you have hidden away on the *T'pau*." The Andorian's blue-tinted face turned even bluer as he gestured wildly. "This is an impossible delay. Besides not having proper instruments for a scientific dig, those Klingons continue to roar and gouge and unsettle everything!"

"Is there indication of seismic disturbance due to their presence?" asked Spock. He gazed impassively at his tricorder. The readout was as firm as bedrock now. No indication of malfunction existed.

"Of course! They do whatever it is they do and set off explosions. Those shock waves can bring the entire cavern roof tumbling down and destroy everything I've worked so hard for."

"Cavern roof? I am afraid I do not understand, Doctor. Are you saying the Klingons are blasting out a cavern?"

"No, no, you . . ." The Andorian bit off his words, realizing it did no good insulting a Vulcan. "I'm convinced," he continued in a conspiratorial whisper, "that the former inhabitants of this planet were not primarily surface dwellers at all. They lived underground in immense caverns. This is why I require all my equipment. I must find that cavern before the Klingons!"

"What evidence leads you to think this?"

"Why, there are not major ruins aboveground, of course," the scientist said, as if lecturing a dimwit. "Any race capable of constructing a pyramid of such advanced design and material would have left much more behind. No indication exists aboveground. Ergo, they lived in subterranean cities!"

"Logical," said Spock, musing over the readings he now received on his tricorder. "My tricorder seems to bear you out. A huge cavity exists approximately fifty point seven three meters under our feet."

"I knew it!" crowed Threllvon-da. "I was right! And I'd have discovered it ever so much sooner if you hadn't lost all my equipment. Let me have that thing. I'll find the proper spot to dig, if the Klingons haven't already located it."

He snatched the tricorder from Spock's hands. The Vulcan started to pull it back, but Lt. Avitts' hand on his arm checked the motion.

"Let him have it, Mr. Spock. You can use mine." She pulled the carrying strap of her tricorder over her head and handed him the device. "It's strange that I didn't get any such reading when I examined the area. I'd've bet the planet was solid mantle for eighty kilometers or more."

"You did not notice the cavern under our feet?" Spock asked, one eyebrow rising slightly. "Fascinating."

"Yes, isn't it?" said Candra Avitts, but just what she found fascinating wasn't immediately apparent. Her eyes never left Spock. He shifted uncomfortably, aware that his renegade emotions were trying to break free again. The nearness of the assistant science officer troubled him greatly in a most un-Vulcanlike manner.

Gruffly, he said, "I wish to observe the Klingon camp."

"The best view is from the side of the pyramid. We've put a ramp up to the entrance." She pointed out the rickety beams tied together with rope leading to the maw of the pyramid. Spock barely noticed as he climbed up to the point where the Klingons were visible over a small rise.

He aimed the tricorder at the equipment and waited for the reading to be digested in the guts of the compact machine. A tiny chuckling noise came from the tricorder. He studied the results and simply stared at the equipment over the hill.

"Is anything wrong, Spock? You seem confused."

"Confused? No, I lack enough information, that's all. My tricorder shows nothing but land-moving equipment. Heavy construction equipment, nothing more. It appears that the Klingons are indeed intent on scientific exploration. Why else use so much heavy equipment of a non-military nature?"

"I tried to check it out," Lt. Avitts said, "but couldn't come to any conclusion. It's all in my report."

"I'm sure it is. No heavy energy weapons detected," he said, continuing to study the readout. "No explosives except those required for blasting out small amounts of the planetary surface. Is there any indication of the weapon used on the *T'pau?*" he asked suddenly.

"No, none," the lieutenant answered. "I thought they might be establishing a base for mounting the weapon, but they're interested only in digging, not in building."

"The readings are strongly indicative that they are over the thinnest portion in the vault of the cavern. Threllvon-da will interpret that to mean they are attempting to steal his discovery of the underground city."

"I never got a reading like that before," confessed the lieutenant. "But does it matter, Spock? Does anything matter—if we are together." She put her hand on his arm and moved disturbingly close.

Spock felt his control slipping away. He turned and looked down into the woman's eyes. Funny, he thought to himself, he had never noticed before how love shone from the eyes. She closed those haunting eyes and parted her lips slightly, waiting in silent expectation.

Like a magnet pulls iron, Spock found himself bending forward to press his lips against Candra Avitts'.

"Spock! Where are you, Spock?" came the querulous voice of Threllvon-da. The mood broken, Spock jerked back guiltily from his assistant, as surprised at his temporary weakness as he was at the guilt-feeling itself.

"Up here, Doctor," he called out, his gaze still on the agitated Candra Avitts. He wanted to reach out and gently touch her, but he didn't. "What is it you require?"

"My equipment! But barring that, I need you to chase off those Klingons. This tricorder of yours tells me that they are over the very spot I've sought for since hitting on the idea of the underground dwellers. They dig at the precise location where the distance is least to penetrate into my city, *my* city! Those bumbling fools will desecrate it. They know nothing of proper scientific technique!"

The short Andorian puffed and panted his way up the ramp until he stood next to Spock and Avitts. He craned his neck and twisted his head around so that his good hearing stalk pointed directly at them.

"Well, what have you to say? Are you going to chase them off, or do I have to go do it myself?"

"I must report to Captain Kirk," said Spock diplomatically, "and shall relay your concern to him. I am sure the captain will know what course of action to follow."

The Andorian went back down the ramp grumbling and muttering to himself. Spock followed, Lt. Avitts disturbingly close to him.

"This is an outrage, Kirk! It means war!" shouted Kalan. He pounded his fist hard enough for sound to reach Kirk, even though no one aboard the *Enterprise* saw what the Klingon captain hit.

Kirk suppressed a smile as he returned the Klingon's furious stare. If Kalan meant what he said, he would have used his phasers rather than the intership communicators. Kalan wanted to negotiate rather than fight. Kirk guessed that even the infamous iron rule aboard the Klingon vessels had failed to maintain adequate control.

Could Kalan fight a successful battle with his crew fomenting mutiny? If even his own daughter plotted against him, Kalan might be in no position to force the issue of Spock's presence on Alnath II.

"Come, come, Captain," said Kirk, beginning to enjoy the exchange. "Mr. Spock's presence on the planet poses no threat whatsoever to your security. What can one man—one Vulcan—do? His mission is peaceful and scientific. We will gladly share the knowledge he has accumulated, since your expedition to Alnath is a scientific one, also."

He gauged the Klingon's response. Storm clouds of anger gathered and were pushed away. Kalan leaned back and pressed a strong fist under his chin as he appraised Kirk.

"Why would we believe you, Kirk? All know of your

treachery. You plot against the security of the Klingon Empire."

"Nonsense, Kalan. All I did was order one man with a tricorder to beam down. Where's the danger in that? Surely, Spock poses no threat to the mighty Klingon dreadnought, *Terror*." He watched Kalan stew at the implied insult.

"No single entity can destroy the pride of the Klingon battle fleet."

"We quite agree, Captain. How can anyone threaten your security?"

"Nonetheless, you should have notified me of this scientific expedition."

"It was of so little consequence I thought it impertinent to annoy you. Besides, this is a free planet, and no Federation citizen or officer requires *your* permission to land." Kirk allowed the proper amount of steel to enter his tones. He had to show Kalan that the *Enterprise* was no paper tiger. The speech had the desired effect. Kalan began to bristle visibly at the implied lack of control the Klingons had over the *Enterprise*.

"You prepare for war even now," accused Kalan, fighting to keep his towering anger under control.

"You are quite wrong, Captain. Perhaps you would care to send a delegation over to the *Enterprise*. We will show you that, while our preparedness is that expected aboard a well-run vessel, we are not making special effort to join battle."

"You'd allow such an inspection?" The Klingon was instantly suspicious. He scowled, trying to think through the possible traps Kirk set. "Very well. I accept. I personally will board with my first officer."

"As you wish, Captain. We will accord you full honors due an equal. Give coordinates for beaming aboard to my transporter chief. Kirk out," he said quickly, before the Klingon replied. Kirk turned to Uhura and ordered, "Block any transporter beam used by the Klingons. I want them to depend entirely on *us*." He settled back in his seat and smiled. Things went well.

"Mr. Chekov, you have the conn. Full honors will be accorded to the Klingon commander while aboard the *Enterprise*. Do I make myself clear?"

"Perfectly, Captain," said Chekov, his voice surly.

"Mr. Chekov, we are not buckling under to the Klingons. This is a move to bring them under our thumbs for a change. Do nothing that will jeopardize that." Seeing no response, Kirk added, "Please remember that diplomacy is using your head without anyone suspecting it."

"Aye, aye, sir," the young ensign said, more cheerfully, but still skeptical of his captain's orders.

Kirk hurried to his cabin and changed into full dress regalia, complete with medals and insignia. While he dressed, he buzzed McCoy on the intercom and told him, "Want you at the transporter on the double, Bones. Full dress uniform. The Klingons are coming aboard."

"Humph," snorted McCoy. "I don't get into that monkey suit for anything short of a court-martial."

"It'll be yours unless you snap to it," said Kirk, smiling. "Bib-overalls are not the dress of the day—yet." He clicked off the intercom and walked briskly to the transporter room. Mr. Kyle had attended to the controls well this time. For that Kirk was glad. This gamble of inviting aboard the Klingons might backfire unless he used their presence to bolster his own position.

"Here they are, sir," said Mr. Kyle reluctantly. He studied the shimmering pillars of energy, judged the proper corrections by eye, then moved the slide controls forward. The columns of energy solidified into two Klingons, both with hands resting on the butts of their sidearms.

"Welcome aboard the *Enterprise*, Captain Kalan," said Kirk. He turned and nodded. Kyle started the shrill recording signifying the ancient custom of piping aboard.

"What is this, Kirk? What manner of trap have you laid for us?"

"Captain Kalan, no trap. None at all." He eyed the Klingon's service uniform with obvious distaste. "Though you certainly came prepared. Do you not wish to die in full dress uniform?"

"I *am* in full dress. We have no need for your decadent frippery," Kalan said haughtily.

"This is my medical officer, Dr. Leonard McCoy," said Kirk, changing the subject abruptly. "And the officer with you is . . .?"

"Lt. Kislath."

The youth sneered openly at both Kirk and McCoy. Kirk responded to the sneer with a friendly smile, while

McCoy did everything possible to hide his distaste, failing miserably in the effort.

"Come, let's explore the *Enterprise*. Or do you prefer refreshment first?"

"The inspection tour," snapped Kalan. "We would see what devil weapons you have hidden."

"Now, if we had such 'devil weapons' we'd hardly show them to you, would we? But we will show you that no unusual preparations have been made. Just standard precautions, nothing more."

"You think this space gas means anything, Captain Kalan?" asked Kislath. "He deceives you. He makes a fool of you."

"Impossible," said Kirk quickly. "No one can make a fool of such a renowned Klingon. I'm surprised that your junior officers entertain such thoughts at all, Kalan. Really." Kirk smiled broadly, and Kalan almost drew his weapon.

"Your phaser banks. We must inspect them."

"Of course. This way, gentlemen."

Kirk did everything he could to create tension between Kislath and Kalan. By the end of the inspection tour of the weapons control area, Kalan had reached the limits of his patience.

"Back to the ship, Kislath. I will speak with you later."

The first officer stiffened and marched off, blazing in anger.

"Those young officers become so ambitious, don't they, Kalan?" McCoy asked, seeing the groundwork Kirk had laid. "I tell you, some of those young bucks working for me need constant watching or they'd have my job in a second, right, Jim?"

"Quite right, Bones. Just the other day I was telling him, Kalan, about one of his med technicians spreading rumors behind his back. We do not tolerate such behavior aboard the *Enterprise*. Not good for morale."

"You executed the man?" asked Kalan, obviously interested. "That is the least punishment that can be given in the Klingon fleet."

"I just gave him a little talking to," said McCoy. "He's a useful man. Our laws hardly permit such extreme punishment."

"But you have need of such?" pressed Kalan. "On a

vessel this size, you must have mutineers constantly plotting."

"We have our ways of thwarting any," assured Kirk. "I doubt if any plot of fewer than, say, twelve conspirators would stand much of a chance." He watched the Klingon's swarthy face cloud over again. Kirk knew exactly what raced through Kalan's mind: the mutiny aboard the *Terror*.

"The only problem with large mutiny attempts," continued Kirk blithely, "is that you can miss tiny cells of discontent. Spreads like cancer."

"That's a neoplasm characterized by—" began McCoy.

"I know what cancer is," growled Kalan. "You have no such problems aboard your vessel?"

"Come, come, Captain. I'd hardly be willing to discuss that with you if I did. But then you can read between the lines. I'd be a fool to invite you aboard the *Enterprise* if there was the slightest hint of discontent."

"Well, Jim," began McCoy, "there is discontent."

"What?" pounced Kalan. "Tell me of it!"

"It's pretty serious," said McCoy, deadpan. "One of the crew actually filed a formal complaint about not being able to get a second dessert. The autochef hadn't prepared enough and the ship's nutrition officer refused to reprogram it for just one more dessert. I tell you, that's the scandal making the rounds of this ship. Rampant discontent."

"No dessert?" said Kalan stupidly. *"That's* the type of trouble you have?"

"We don't want to discuss such a serious matter now, Doctor," said Kirk sternly. "Dismissed. I will speak with you later."

"No dessert?" repeated Kalan.

"Is there anything else you wish to see, Captain?" asked Kirk. "We don't have anything to hide. I trust you are convinced that everything is shipshape aboard the *Enterprise* and, while we maintain top readiness, we are not going to provoke an incident in violation of the Organian Peace Treaty."

"I shall consider what I have seen," said Kalan stiffly. "I demand to return to my ship."

"At once. This way, Captain."

Kirk watched the Klingon enter the transporter booth, turn into the scintillant, coruscating column of energy, then vanish. He heaved a sigh of relief and leaned back against the transporter console.

"How'd it go, Jim?" asked McCoy, coming into the room.

"Just fine, Bones. Kalan's seen that we're ready to fight —and he thinks we're at top readiness. He knows the condition of his own crew. He won't try anything, not until he has reinforcements, and I think he's too proud to ask for any. After all, he has the best ship in the Klingon fleet. He can't admit the *Enterprise* poses any sort of a problem for him."

"Young Kislath presents a huge problem for him, though," observed McCoy. "He's likely to toss Kislath into the brig, just on general principles."

"I hope so. The more distrust among them, the stronger we look in comparison. It's a good thing they don't know the true extent of our discipline problems. And that story about the missed dessert was a brilliant lie, Bones."

"It wasn't a lie, Jim. It actually happened."

"It did?" The confidence Kirk had felt drained and left him feeling old and tired. It would be a long time before he found a solution to this knotty problem.

Chapter Six

Captain's Log: Stardate 4735.7

The Klingons attempted another subspace communication. My encounter with Kalan aboard the *Enterprise* has borne fruit. He has found more mutineers and executed them. As a result, I feel that the safety of the *Enterprise* and the Andorian archaeological team is enhanced. However, no progress has been made toward solving the mystery of the Klingon weapon which has killed the Vulcans aboard the *T'pau.* I can only hope that the weapon requires the coordinated effort of many Klingons rather than the action of a single one.

"Kirk, the equipment you furnished me is substandard. I refuse to work with it." The blue-faced Andorian tilted his broken stalk away from Kirk and quivered with rage.

"Dr. Threllvon-da, please let me explain," began Kirk. He paused, took a deep breath, ordered his thoughts and then launched into his explanation. "We cannot simply leave orbit and recover the *T'pau's* stores. This would leave the Klingon ship in control of the planet. The shuttle craft are not equipped to make the journey. Besides that, I don't want to bring the *T'pau* back into orbit around Alnath. As long as it is drifting on a vector only we know, it remains a potential explanation for the Klingon weapon."

"Weapon, weapon, you're always ranting about this

so-called weapon. What do I care? I'm a scientist and I dig in the ground. To dig I need something more than my talons." He held up gnarled hands. "I need my equipment, and you're keeping me from it."

"Believe me, Doctor, if there was any way I could send you out after it, I would in a nanosecond. But the equipment furnished from the *Enterprise* is adequate for the task. Spock has assured me—"

"Spock! That bungler!"

Kirk fell speechless for a moment. No one had ever called Spock a bungler before. The Vulcan might be many things, but not inept.

"What do you mean?"

"I mean what I say. He completely lost a full day's seismic data acquired with your primitive equipment. He and that lumpy female—Avitts I think's the name—were mooning and carrying on so, he accidentally erased the data tape. I took over the monitoring myself after chasing him out of my sight, of course."

"Yes, of course," said Kirk. "That's not like Spock."

"I want into that subterranean city before the Klingons, Kirk, and I don't care how I do it. If you train your phasers on coordinates I give you, we can blast—"

"NO!"

"Be reasonable, Kirk. You keep me from my equipment and now you refuse me this one little request. A one-second blasting will take me down into the cavern ahead of the Klingons. I must beat them. *I must!*"

"I'll see what can be done. First, I must talk with my science officer."

"Good," said Threllvon-da. "Anything to keep him from my precious data. Anything!"

Spock's eyes were unfocused, and his mind wandered. The tricorder readings went unobserved. Only the sudden buzz from the device brought him back to his senses. He looked down at the tricorder as if seeing it for the first time. The information on its display screen was alien to him. For a span of several heartbeats he was unable to remember what he had been doing.

Then it all rushed back to him. The seismic readings. Threllvon-da needed them to direct the excavations. The Andorian didn't want to bring the roof of the cavern crashing down onto his subterranean city. And Spock had once again failed to obtain the proper data.

"Is anything wrong, Spock?" asked Candra Avitts.

The woman's nearness bothered him. He pulled away to keep her from touching him. Her perfume was decidedly non-regulation; it aroused him. The sight of her lustrous hair falling in a wild cascade around her creamy shoulders made him aware of intense desires within himself. Her beauty had gone unnoticed too long. He had to have her. He needed her desperately.

His hands reached out to take hold of her trim body, then he stopped.

His mind reeled. This was emotional behavior, he told himself. This wasn't the way a Vulcan acted. Centuries ago they had expunged emotion from their psyches in an attempt to do away with devastating war and wanton killing. On Vulcan, it had worked. A doctrine of absolute peace required emotionless analysis of every situation.

Violence was not out of the question when self-defense required it. Only the emotionless, logic-directed mind could evaluate those rare circumstances properly. Emotion was a killer. He dared not succumb to Candra Avitts' beauty. That would kindle the fires of emotional involvement and lead down the path denied to all Vulcans a millennium and more ago.

"Please leave me alone, Lieutenant. I need time to think."

"Spock, you don't look well. Let me get Dr. McCoy."

"The doctor knows little of Vulcan physiology. Dr. M'Benga is the one trained in such matters."

"M'Benga, then. Are you all right?" Concern shone in her eyes, concern for him. Spock was touched. No one had cared for him in this way before. He fought down the incipient emotion of love, of caring, of cherishing another without recourse to logic.

"I am not ill. I require time to meditate."

"I . . . I'll be nearby, Spock. If you need me, just call."

"I have my communicator. And I will not require your assistance, Lieutenant. Might I suggest you aid Dr. Threllvon-da until I require your services again?"

"Dr. Threllvon-da can handle this stage of the seismic testing by himself," said Avitts, still worried about Spock. She started to take a step toward him, then froze. The look in his eyes told her that this was not the place for her. Reluctantly, she left the small hut, glancing back only once to see the impassive Mr. Spock sitting in the center of the floor, legs crossed and eyelids lowered.

The Vulcan meditated. He felt himself floating between worlds, soaring from sun to sun, drifting on the solar winds, plunging down into gravity wells and racing back into space. His body relaxed. The beating of his heart slowed until only a doctor trained in Vulcan anatomy could have detected a pulse.

His mind quieted and the disturbing emotions he had felt were eradicated. And once eliminated, the cause was examined in minute detail. Physical attraction? Absurd. It led only to jealousy and mind-twisting love. Discard it. Love? Only a name humans attached to a madness that seized them. *Pon farr* was on them continuously. An illogical way of administering to the needs of a race. The seven year cycle was more logical.

Logic.

Quiet.

Meditative techniques a half million years old soothed his mind, allowed it to operate as it had been trained. His half-human part had begun to intrude in ways not to his liking. He knew the only recourse for preventing further recurrences: complete and total logic. He must become a living, breathing computer. He must weigh every decision only in the light of logic. If the data furnished him was insufficient, so be it. He would not extrapolate. In that way lay the madness of humanity. Extrapolation colored reality with hope, with ambition, with other more heinous emotions felt only by humans.

He denied all emotion.

The coldness descended on him. The coldness—and a tiny spot of brilliance more blinding than a star. Spock's mind pounced on it, coaxed it, tried to lure it closer for examination. The point danced and darted just out of his reach.

Even in the depths of his meditation, his heart began to speed at the sight of that point of light. In it lay the answers to all questions in the universe. His mind reached out hungrily for it. The spot vanished. He calmed himself, denied the emotion of curiosity, regained the point of light. It drifted ever nearer promising fulfillment of all his dreams. If he could only touch it! His mind went out, narrowed, missed the point and circled around.

It was maddeningly close!

Again the surge of emotion drove away the one thing in the universe most enticing to him. Spock concentrated on that dot of light and it came closer. No emotion marred his mental perfection. He might have been some flesh and blood computer just activated. The spot bounced millimeters—and light-years—away. All space concentrated in that point. All time. All.

The answers to ultimate questions came to him. His mind recoiled from the immensity of those answers. His logic manipulated and turned the information over and over. He understood. More, he *understood*.

No question went unanswered in his mind. He was a god. His mind reached out to the alien point of light to merge with it, to achieve the next logical step in evolution.

The fringes of his groping mental probe touched the spot. Triumph surged in Spock's breast.

The point exploded with the fury of a sun going nova. The Vulcan fell backward, stunned. Opening his eyes revealed only the roof of the primitive hut. The light was gone. The promise of total knowledge had been ripped away from his grip at the last moment due to his damnable emotion of triumph. Even deep in his meditative trance he failed to keep out human emotion.

Spock cried bitter tears. Unashamed, he let them streak down his cheeks. Sobbing, he rolled onto his belly and pounded clenched fists into the soft dirt as he vented his rage. Only slowly did his anger and frustration come under conscious control.

The Vulcan straightened, dusted off his uniform and went outside. The bright sun made him squint, but the intense yellow sunlight appeared only a candle in the dark compared to the light of knowledge that had almost been his.

"Mr. Spock?" asked Lt. Avitts anxiously. "I heard noises from inside the hut. It sounded like . . . crying. Are you all right?"

"You can see that I am, Lieutenant. Might I suggest you attend to your duties and stop interfering in my personal affairs? That is the most efficient course of action for all of us."

"I'm sorry, Spock. I didn't mean anything by it."

"Report to Dr. Threllvon-da and inform him I am

beaming back aboard the *Enterprise*. I have acquired another bit of information that Captain Kirk requires."

"Aye, aye, sir," the lieutenant said doubtfully. She stood and watched as the transporter beam seized hold of Spock's molecular structure, defied quantum physics and the Heisenberg Principle and sucked him up into the orbiting spaceship. Sadly, she turned and paced off to find the Andorian scientist.

"Here he is, Jim," said McCoy, leaning against the transporter console and skeptically examining the flashing lights. "He made it intact. Or so I guess. Damn machine might have jumbled up his internal organs, though with the way Spock's put together, no one'd know the difference."

"Your comments are highly illogical, Doctor," said Spock stiffly. "If my internal arrangement has been altered by the transporter, this would cause a change in function. Enzymes normally produced would be subverted and amino acid levels altered. Your statement, just examining the most obvious items, is fallacious."

"Spock, were you born without a sense of humor or did you have it surgically removed?"

"Enough, Bones. Report, Mr. Spock. I'm interested in hearing about the Klingon presence on the planet."

The trio walked out into the hall and down the corridor until they came to a wardroom. Chasing several junior officers out for the sake of privacy, Spock began his report.

"I can add little to what is known, Captain. The Klingons are performing certain mining operations at the exact point Threllvon-da has determined to be the weakest, least thick spot of the cavern roof. They will break through shortly."

"I can't believe it, Jim," said McCoy. "The Klingons aren't interested in archaeology."

"Unless they hope to learn something of great value," said Spock. "I have had an experience which might relate to that."

"You mean you've finally seen how attractive Lt. Avitts is?' 'said McCoy, grinning with wicked glee. "I figured it'd take awhile but I was willing to wait and see what type of female penetrated that icy, logical facade of yours."

"I . . . I find Lt. Avitts attractive," said Spock, his voice almost a whisper. Kirk sat on the edge of his seat, leaning forward when he heard the confession. Even McCoy was taken aback by the straightforward declaration. "However, that is not what I wish to report."

"Why not?" said McCoy. "I call this a day of celebration. You've finally admitted there's a human side to your damnable logic. Celebrate, Spock, rejoice! You'll learn to be free of the shackles of total logic and maybe one day even get rid of those computers you insist on communing with all the time."

"Doctor, I am well aware of the discrepancies in my personal behavior. The emotional outbursts appall me. Even the idea of being appalled is in direct contradiction to my normal mode of behavior. I must point out, in all fairness, your own behavior is less than normal."

"Mine?" snorted McCoy. "I'm fine. Nothing wrong with me. It's those machines. I'm finally breaking free of their tyranny. I want the simple life. . . ."

"You make my case for me, Doctor. At no time have you ever been the servant of a machine. You are always the master; however, you have become pathological in your distrust of machines. This aspect of your personality has come boiling to the surface only since we achieved orbit around Alnath II. Likewise, the crew is not performing at calculated levels."

"Are you able to pinpoint the cause, Spock? If so, I've got to know. I'm tearing my hair out trying to get the *Enterprise* one hundred percent efficient."

"I am aware of that, Captain. I have no further evidence of radiations or fields emanating from the planet. A computer surveillance is continuing, but appears futile at this time."

"What are you saying, Spock? This planet is driving us space happy and you don't know why?" Kirk pounded his fist against the table. Information! He needed information and was thwarted on every attempt at obtaining it. Even his efficient science officer had been stymied.

"I have nothing to report on that, Captain. As I was saying before Dr. McCoy interrupted, I had an emotional seizure and required time to meditate. As I did so, I *saw* a tiny point of brilliance."

"You *saw* it?" asked Kirk. "The way you say it makes it sound as if you didn't see it with your eyes."

"That is essentially correct, Captain. I *saw* it with my

inner vision. My mind power, perhaps, or whatever you wish to call it."

"Metaphysical claptrap is what I call it," scoffed McCoy.

"Vulcans have more convolutions in the cortex of the brain than do humans, Doctor. Integral with this added complexity is a power of the mind not shared with humans. I *saw*." Spock lapsed into silence as he composed himself. Kirk watched the calming effect of whatever mental discipline the Vulcan applied.

"It was that disturbing?" Kirk finally asked.

"Yes, Captain. Disturbing and yet . . . appealing. I have no words for it. I *felt* that my innermost dreams would come true if I made mental contact with that spot of light. I reached out mentally and attempted to touch it, but at the last moment before contact a surge of emotion drove it away."

"Was it alive?"

Spock shook his head, a sad expression coming over him. "I cannot say. I doubt it, yet there were certain life-qualities about it. If only I hadn't reacted emotionally."

"Like you are now, Spock," said Kirk sharply. "Describe in detail this spot of light. Could it be a pure energy life-form we have failed to discover on the planet? Is this the cause of the crews unrest?"

"Negative, sir. I felt as if the spot came from within my brain, not from outside. It had to be something caused—controlled—by me and me alone."

"This isn't a Klingon mind-control device?" pressed Kirk. "We still have no inkling what they did to the Vulcan science ship crew. Are they focusing some sort of mental image and scrambling our heads?"

"Illogical, Captain. Kalan appears to have discipline problems of an even graver nature aboard the *Terror*. If this so-called mind-control weapon is operating, it isn't being used by the Klingons. Or rather, it is being used against them, also."

"The key word is 'appears,' Spock. How do we really know that Kalan has any problems at all? The transmissions might be ruses. Perhaps he hasn't executed anyone for mutiny, much less his own daughter. Lt. Kislath's behavior and Kalan's suspicions while aboard the *Enterprise* might be an act for our benefit."

"But they hold the full house, Jim," pointed out Mc-

Coy. "Didn't you say the *Terror* is more powerful? If they opened fire on us, they'd blow us to atoms in a few minutes. They didn't attack the Andorians either when they had the chance."

"Dammit!" flared Kirk. "The longer this drags on, the more confused it gets. What are the Klingons doing on Alnath? What is it that killed those Vulcans? What, what, *what?*"

"That is a good question, Captain," said Spock solemnly.

Kirk turned and balled his fists, wanting to strike out. Only an intense act of willpower prevented him from hitting his first officer.

"Ensign Chekov," called Lt. Uhura, "I'm getting another transmission from the Klingon vessel."

"Decode the message," Chekov ordered. He moved to the captain's command seat and swiveled around, surveying the readiness of the bridge. All went quietly about their duties. He felt puffed with pride. He had been able to keep them at peak efficiency while Captain Kirk had failed. Ambition burned brightly in Chekov's breast. A good report and he would make lieutenant in record time.

No longer Ensign Chekov but Lieutenant Chekov. But why stop there? Commander Chekov! Even Starship Captain Chekov!

He would do his duty well. He would be decisive and act responsibly to maintain the safety of the *Enterprise* and the Federation.

"It's encoded with a different sequence, Ensign," said the communications officer. "The computer is working. The decoding will take a few minutes."

"Very well." He leaned back and stared at the viewscreen. The Klingon vessel poised just above the horizon, bright and ominous. One single command aboard that ship and the *Enterprise* would come under furious attack, an attack the smaller cruiser might not withstand. That dare not happen. He, Chekov, must be the first to discover if the Klingons sought teachery and death—or peace.

But he didn't kid himself for an instant. Klingons were incapable of desiring peace. They were warlike, mercenary, cold-blooded. Dealing with them was only a little safer than playing Russian roulette with a hand phaser.

Kill or be killed. That was the only credo the Klingons believed in. Chekov would not be caught napping while in command of the *Enterprise*. On his shoulders rested the final decision to launch a preemptive attack or not. All the senior officers were concerned with other matters. The Captain sought answers to the Vulcans' deaths, Spock scrabbled in the ruins of the planet below for the same answers. Commander Scott fiddled with his engines, and Sulu was off duty. Command was Pavel Chekov's.

"Decoding complete," sang out Uhura. "It's another report tagged with 'highest priority.'"

"Skip any inconsequential details. Give me only the meat of the message," he ordered.

"Aye, aye, Ensign," said Uhura, pressing the ear receiver in more fully to listen to the intercepted Klingon message. "It's sent to their home base. It says that efficiency is dwindling, that they are resisting, more execution, many in the brig. They . . . it's garbled, Ensign."

Chekov's eyes glazed over. Trouble brewing aboard the Klingon vessel. What would be their most likely course of action? To fire on the *Enterprise!* It had to be. The Klingons never tolerated being second best. They planned to attack before the *Enterprise* realized their diabolical intentions. Chekov knew that had to be the content of the message.

"It's clearer now. The computer has refined some of the decoding. It . . . no, it can't be!" cried Uhura, eyes widening in horror.

"They attack soon," said Chekov flatly, certain of his conclusions.

"Yes, that's it! They're preparing to attack!"

"Battle stations," commanded Chekov. He came fully alive now. He felt in the center of a giant web of nerve endings, all pulsing and sparking with life. The lightest twitch on his part caused ripples to flow along the strands of that web and produced instant action at the perimeters.

The loud clanging filled the ship. Chekov felt the adrenaline pumping through his arteries. Never before in his life had he felt this alive, this powerful, this sure of his own actions.

"All hands to battle stations," repeated Chekov. "Phasers prepare to fire. Track Klingon vessel. Photon torpedoes load!"

"Chekov," shouted Uhura over the din of the bridge,

"are you sure of what you're doing? Shouldn't you call Captain Kirk?"

"No time. Message said to attack us. Such a powerful ship can destroy us with little effort—unless we attack first. I will do so as soon as the phaser banks are charged and ready."

The lights on the command console blinked menacingly, showing full phaser charge. The young ensign quickly ran through the checklist in his mind. Phasers charged. Tracking computers locked on target. Photon torpedoes ready to follow up the first phaser barrage, to give the Klingons something to think about while the phaser banks charged again.

"What's the meaning of this?" came the sharp question from the door of the turbo-elevator. "Explain yourself, Mr. Chekov!"

"Captain! He's ordered an attack," cried Uhura.

"All hands, as you were. I say again, as you were. There is no, repeat, *no* attack being launched from the *Enterprise*. This is Captain Kirk. All weapons systems to be placed in Readiness Condition Two, repeating, Condition Two."

The red-faced captain spun and faced the ensign. "Mr. Chekov, I thought we had an understanding. Nothing of this sort was to happen if I gave you the conn. Explain your actions to me and perhaps you won't have to do so at a court-martial board."

"Lt. Uhura intercepted another Klingon message, Captain," the ensign said, his voice trembling. He locked himself rigidly at attention and stared straight ahead. "They planned a sneak attack on *Enterprise*. I acted only to save the ship." The young ensign couldn't control the nervous shaking that wracked his body.

Kirk took a deep breath and settled down into his command seat. His fingers raced across the tiny console, his eyes darting from station to station on the bridge, until he assured himself that no hothead was going to press the firing trigger on one of the phasers. He took another deep breath and turned his attention to Ensign Chekov.

"No matter what the content of the message, your duty was to inform me. You are the most junior officer in the chain of command on this bridge. I considered it valuable experience for you to have conn time. You had no right to make such a decision."

"Begging your pardon, sir. If I had the conn, I was acting captain of *Enterprise*. You gave me authority to act in the ship's best interests."

"He is right, Captain," said Mr. Spock. "Regulation Seven, subparagraph three clearly states that—"

"Enough, Mr. Spock. I am well aware of the regulations. But you, Mr. Chekov, overstepped the bounds of your position."

"Yes, sir."

"Lt. Uhura, read the message that almost got us killed." Kirk controlled his rage. Looking around, he saw many on the bridge silently siding with Chekov. They wanted action. Kirk knew he kept them checked, their violent impulses under strict control. Chekov had almost loosed the dogs of war. Turning to Spock he saw nothing but the impassive expression. Sometimes he envied the Vulcan, especially at times like this.

". . . request for immediate attack," finished Uhura.

"The message is incontrovertible, Captain," said Spock. "The Klingons requested permission to attack us."

"Uhura," asked Kirk, drowning out Spock's comment, "did that transmission get through our jamming?"

"No, sir. There is only a slight chance it punched through as far as the edge of this solar system, some ten light-hours distant. Unless the Klingons have a relay placed in a location as yet undetected, they did not reach their home base."

"Thank you, Lieutenant. Did you consider that, Mr. Chekov, before you ordered general quarters?"

"No, sir. But—"

"Mr. Spock, analyze the wording and content of the message. Take into account the type of code used in the transmission."

"Hmmm, most interesting, Captain. From the syntax of the message and the encoding, I'd venture the opinion that Kalan did not send it."

"What?" cried Chekov, taking a half-step forward. "How can that be? It came from the Klingon ship!"

"Exactly, Ensign. From the Klingon ship, but not necessarily from Captain Kalan." Kirk slumped into the seat. "The *Terror* has been in the throes of constant mutiny since orbiting Alnath II. I believe this was sent by someone under Kalan desiring to take over command, but is attempting to do so in more orthodox and less mutinous ways."

"An end run," exclaimed Uhura. "Someone is trying to get the approval of their base to attack us and oust Kalan in the process."

"That is the way I read this data, Lieutenant. Mr. Spock, do you concur?"

"It has a high probability, Captain. I would add further that the most likely candidate for this 'end run,' as Lt. Uhura called it, is Kislath."

"The Klingon did show a considerable amount of rebellious spirit," agreed Kirk. "My plan for disrupting their fighting efficiency seems to be paying dividends. And you jeopardized it, Mr. Chekov. Any words in your own defense?"

"No, sir." Chekov braced again, his face pale.

"You are confined to your quarters until further notice, Mr. Chekov. Dismissed."

Kirk watched the ensign smartly pivot and march from the bridge. He felt something inside him go cold as he realized how near they had all been to another interstellar war.

"This can't go on, Spock," he said heatedly. "I didn't do enough when I planted the seeds of doubt in Kislath's mind. I didn't do enough turning Kalan against him. If something's not done fast, we're all going to be radioactive dust floating among the stars."

"If we are lucky, that is," said Spock. Kirk stared at him as Spock added, "We might live to see the devastation of war."

Chapter Seven

Captain's Log: Stardate 4736.0

Ensign Chekov's action will be reviewed by the senior officers aboard the *Enterprise*. If they so recommend, a general court-martial will be convened when —if—we return to Starbase. I sympathize with Chekov; I feel he had only the best interests of the ship at heart. However, he failed to adequately analyze the situation and nearly plunged the Federation into a brutal, no-winner interstellar war with the Klingon Empire.

"The Board of Inquiry is hereby convened," intoned Kirk, picking up a small mallet and ringing an ancient seafaring ship's bell three times. "Is the defendant present?"

Chekov stood to attention.

"Do you request legal assistance during this hearing? Such is your right. However, I must point out that no criminal charges will be heard at this time."

"No counsel is required."

"So be it."

Kirk glanced up and down the table in the wardroom. At the far end sat McCoy, looking grim. Next to him sat Scott, a worried look on his face. Lt. Patten of Security sat on the far side of Spock. Kirk turned his attention back to Chekov.

"The charges are serious, Ensign. While technically you

were in command of the ship and entrusted with responding to any emergency, subsequent study of the Klingon transmission and analysis of the situation shows no imminent danger to the *Enterprise*. In such an instance, you are required to call a ranking command officer. You failed to do so. Are there any extenuating circumstances this board should be apprised of?"

"No, sir." Chekov stood bravely, waiting for the verdict. If he was lucky, the discipline would be slight. A notation of incompetence would be entered in his record followed by a drumming out of the fleet. If he wasn't lucky, the court-martial would convene at Starbase and find him guilty of a command error. He'd spend the rest of his life on a prison asteroid worrying over the single mistake that had put him there.

"I wish to enter extenuating testimony into the records, Captain," said Spock.

Kirk looked up, surprised. "Very well, Mr. Spock. Computer, please record and evaluate."

"Working," came the feminine voice from the computer console.

"I have recently spent several planetary rotations on the surface of Alnath II attempting to determine any adverse factors in the makeup of the planet," Spock began. "I failed to reach any scientifically defensible conclusions; however, I feel that certain statements stand on their own due to empirical observations."

"He *feels?*" said McCoy, under his breath. "This is a new one. I'm glad the computer's recording this. I want copies."

Kirk silenced the doctor with a glare. "Proceed, Mr. Spock. And please remember that personal feelings are not admissible evidence for this hearing."

"I understand, Captain. While I failed to find the source of the field or fields of unknown origin, duration and composition, there can be no denying the fact that the crew of the *Enterprise*—and, ostensibly, of the Klingon ship, *Terror*—has behaved in atypical fashion since attaining orbit of Alnath.

"The reasons for this are not discernible yet. The effect of the planetary system is obvious. Each crew member has attempted, with varying degrees of success, to pursue whatever course of action that is personally most satisfying. Mr. Kyle, the transporter chief, had an unblemished record until he left his post, without authorization, to sculpt. Commander Scott," Spock continued, staring at the engineer, "has become obsessed with fine-tuning the warp engines."

"Mr. Spock, you canna know what yer sayin'!" Scotty cried. "Those engines needed work, mon. They still do."

"Computer," continued Spock impassively. "Status on warp-drive engines."

"Working," said the computer. "The engines are presently functioning at one hundred seven percent of normal capacity."

"A seven percent improvement over norm," pointed out Spock. "Computer, status report concerning the engines prior to current modifications."

"Working. The engines were performing at one hundred one percent of Starfleet norm."

"Mr. Scott has always maintained the engines of this ship in more than adequate condition. The computer verifies that."

"But they need more!"

"Only in your mind, Mr. Scott. Your need to further augment the function of the warp engines is relatively harmless. Dr. McCoy, on the other hand, has forsaken the use of his medical computer and other advanced surgical equipment, preferring to rely instead on primitive methods."

"Machines turned on me."

"Indeed, Doctor, did they 'turn on you' or have you somehow managed to cause them to malfunction as a result of your basic distrust of all mechanisms?"

"Mr. Spock, is this germane to Ensign Chekov's dereliction of duty?"

"It is, Captain. Even I have not been immune from whatever force is acting on all living things in this system. I do not say 'pernicious force' because, as in the case of Mr. Scott, beneficial results have occurred. For the most part, however, the crew of the *Enterprise* has not functioned as a unit at peak efficiency. Computer, efficiency status of crew since attaining orbit around Alnath II."

"Working. Efficiency is down nineteen percent."

"Our last efficiency report stated the *Enterprise* had the second highest performance rating in the entire fleet. This decline in efficiency puts us in the lowest ranks."

"Mr. Spock, I again remind you that the *Enterprise*

and its senior officers are not the subject of this hearing. Ensign Chekov is. Please be brief." Kirk heaved a sigh and prayed that Spock could summon up enough evidence to get Chekov off the hook.

"Ensign Chekov is human; likewise, he is affected by this empirically demonstrable, if scientifically unknown, force acting upon us. His only crime is being too conscientious in carrying out his duties. He saw a Klingon message that he interpreted as menacing the safety of the *Enterprise.* He acted. His brashness was accentuated by the force. Mr. Chekov, under other circumstances, without the influence of this unknown force, might have acted more responsibly. In my opinion as science officer, he is not culpable in this instance."

Spock quickly sat down. Kirk glanced back at Chekov. The ensign still held himself in a stiff parade-ground brace.

"Computer," asked Kirk, "analysis of Mr. Spock's data."

"Data has not been given," primly informed the computer. "Only personal observation and speculation."

"This is not as easy as it seemed," said Kirk. "I am inclined to agree with Mr. Spock concerning the ensign's actions. This force, whatever it is, adversely affected Mr. Chekov's decision-making faculties at a critical moment. How does the Board vote in this matter? For court-martial, for disciplinary action at command level or dismissal of charges?"

"Dismissal," promptly said Lt. Patten. "Aye, dismissal," said Scott a fraction of a second later. McCoy nodded assent. Spock's decision was obvious.

"Very well. This Board of Inquiry finds that while Ensign Pavel Chekov did not act in the best interests of either the Federation or the Starship *Enterprise,* such action did not stem from personal error. Rather, this . . . malaise . . . aboard the *Enterprise* takes many forms. This is one. Recommendation of the Captain: charges dismissed. Further recommendation: more careful observation and greater thought to be applied to issues confronting us."

Kirk stood and picked up the mallet to strike the bell. "This Board of Inquiry is adjourned." Before he rang the bell, the intercom whined and Uhura's anxious voice sounded.

"Emergency, Captain. Threllvon-da reports that the

Klingons are attempting to seize the ground party by force."

"To the bridge. You, too, Chekov," he said as he hurried from the room. His senior officers quickly returned to their stations. Chekov might have endangered them with his actions; the Klingons had acted as the young ensign had feared.

Kirk slipped into his command seat and barked, "Full vision, Uhura. I will speak directly to Threllvon-da."

"Aye, aye, sir."

The screen blurred, then hardened into a crisp picture. The broken ear stalk of the Andorian filled the viewscreen until the scientist moved away. His blue-tinted face had drained to an unhealthy lavender.

"Captain Kirk! They landed in force. They seized my crew. They . . . they . . ."

"Please, Doctor, tell me exactly what happened. Are you in personal danger at this moment? We'll beam you up if you are."

"No, no, I've locked myself in the communications shed. They've not found me yet. They came in those huge excavating machines. The first ones they captured were your crew members."

"Candra!" cried Spock, stepping forward. Kirk saw the horrified expression on the Vulcan's face. The clenched hands, the slight sheen of sweat on his face, the stark concern were atypical of the first officer.

"Did the Klingons harm them? Or any of your crew?"

"I don't think so. I saw them herding everyone at phaserpoint, but everyone was walking. No injuries, at least no serious ones. Kirk, you've got to stop them!"

"At ease, Doctor. I'll see what can be done. Remain in the shed and keep us posted. Lt. Uhura will stay in constant communication with you. This is being recorded and prepared for Starfleet Command. Any breach of the Organian Peace Treaty will be fully documented."

"Captain, beam me down," said Spock urgently. "Please!"

"Spock, there's nothing you can do down there. You are more valuable to the *Enterprise*—and Lt. Avitts—where you are." Kirk bit down on his knuckle as his mind raced, discarding potential courses of action, considering others.

"Lt. Uhura, maintain the com-link with the planet.

Patch me in on a subchannel to the *Terror*. I want to speak to Kalan."

Uhura efficiently established the necessary link. The dour commander of the Klingon vessel appeared. It didn't take a telepath to realize the towering anger filling the alien captain.

"Kirk! This is war!" he raged.

"I might say the same, Kalan," said Kirk coldly. "Kidnapping my crew members, threatening a peaceful, unarmed archaeological party, illegal seizure of Federation property and—"

"And nothing!" raged the Klingon. "The Andorian caused this!"

"Captain Kalan," Kirk replied so quietly that the Klingon had to lower his own voice to hear. "Let's meet and discuss this."

"Not aboard the *Enterprise*. I will not be taken prisoner by a devious, self-seeking pirate such as yourself."

"Nor will I board the *Terror*. Since the surface of Alnath II appears to be as close to neutral territory as we have, let's meet there—with a maximum of three advisors —in one hour, standard."

"Done," sneered Kalan. His swarthy face clouded further as he added, "And no tricks. If there is a hint of treachery on your part, the *Terror* will blow you from the skies!"

The picture dissolved. Kirk shook his head. "At least he didn't start firing. That's something. I just wonder how much."

"Very well," said Kirk, cinching the belt tightly around his middle. He checked the positioning of the phaser and communicator. "I'll maintain constant contact, Mr. Spock. I want the entire meeting recorded."

"The Klingon jamming of subspace communications will not adversely affect the laser com-link. The laser will pick up any and all broadcasts."

"Good. You're in command, Spock. Are the rest of you ready?" Kirk turned and looked at Chekov, who nervously shuffled from foot to foot, and to McCoy, uneasy about the prospect of stepping into the transporter.

"Isn't there a safer way, Jim? Like the shuttle. We could take it down into the atmosphere and—"

"Into the transporter, Bones. Mr. Spock will oversee the transmission."

"That's what I'm afraid of," he said glumly. The doctor moved hesitantly, as if his feet had turned into lumps of pure neutronium. He positioned himself under one of the transporter electrodes and said, "Hurry it up. I want to get this over as soon as possible. Keep me here another ten seconds and I'll lose my nerve."

Chekov laughed and discreetly hid his smile behind a hand and a feigned cough. He stood ramrod straight just as the transporter energized. In less time than the transition of an electron from one quantum level to another, they reappeared on the surface of Alnath II.

"Ensign," warned Kirk, seeing Chekov reaching for his phaser. "This is a peaceful mission. Keep that combative spirit of yours under closer scrutiny."

"Aye, aye, sir," he said reluctantly. His eyes fastened on the small knot of Klingons lounging arrogantly at the base of the ebony pyramid.

"Captain Kalan, welcome to Alnath II," Kirk said lightly, his hand outstretched. He held it for a moment, then retracted it after the Klingon made no move to shake hands.

"It is I who welcomes you, Kirk. We now possess this planet. I claim it as part of the Klingon Empire."

"Can't be done, Kalan," said Kirk forcefully. "We were here first. Not the *Enterprise*, of course, but the Vulcan science ship and the expedition aboard it."

"Bring forth the Vulcans who claimed this planet."

"You murderous swine! You killed them. For a dreadnought as powerful as yours, it was like dynamiting fish in a barrel," snapped McCoy.

Kalan seemed taken aback by the outburst. "We have done nothing," he said. "These Vulcans died in space. We know nothing of them. All the Empire chooses to acknowledge is our claim to this planet. We have done what is required. A settlement, thirty planetary rotations in residence, the formal claims—all done."

"The Andorians were here before you. Which brings up the question of Dr. Threllvon-da. Where is he?"

"How should I know what has become of those backstabbing—"

Kalan's sentence was cut off by the snappish tones of the Andorian scientist. "I am here, Kirk. And you came in good time. He didn't have the chance to murder me in my sleep like he did the others."

Kislath reached for his phaser but Chekov was faster. The young ensign's grip on the Klingon's wrist tightened like titanium steel. He forced the Klingon officer to release his hold on the butt of his phaser.

"Threllvon-da, please explain what happened to your digging crew."

"*They* came and took them at phaserpoint, that's what happened to them," the scientist accused breathlessly. The blue color of his face heightened with emotion. "They dragged them off and killed them."

"They are merely imprisoned for violating Klingon space," said Kalan. "As you will be imprisoned if you do not leave. This planet is ours!"

"You pose a sticky problem, Kalan," said Kirk, his mind racing over the facts of colonization as he knew them. "What we have is misinterpretation of the agreed upon terms of colonization. As long as Threllvon-da is here and performing archaeological studies on a prior civilization, the evidence for which you plainly see behind you, the planet is *not* fair game. Look it up."

One of the Klingons pressed close to Kalan and whispered hurriedly. The expression on the Klingon's face told Kirk he had won his point. He didn't give the Klingon a chance to think of new devilment.

"And I demand to see my crew, improperly imprisoned, it seems. But their safe return will be sufficient. And, of course, the return of the digging crew."

"They trespassed onto our space," snapped Kislath. "They came into our compound and began digging, as if this wasn't enough for them." He pointed to the area around the base of the pyramid already excavated by Threllvon-da.

"Doctor, is that true?"

"We have to reach the subterranean city before they do. And you refused to get us our equipment. I can't have these blundering fools smashing through the vault of the city and raining down tons of debris. It would ruin the archaeological value of the city for all time!"

"So you did enter the Klingon camp?" asked Kirk.

"Yes, of course. And then these barbarians came over and killed all my crew."

"The humans and the Andorians are not dead. We imprisoned them for trespassing on Klingon territory."

"We've already established that this isn't part of the Klingon Empire," said Kirk sternly. "It does seem, however, you have a claim against the Federation due to the intrusion of some of its citizens to dig in spots within your compound." As Kalan puffed up with victory, Kirk hurried on. "And such claim, of course, is now voided because of your intrusion into *this* camp and kidnapping the Federation citizens who did not take part in the original trespass."

"But—"

"I think an equitable solution is apparent. You give back all the captured scientists—and members of the *Enterprise* crew—and we will not pursue this matter further."

"That makes us come out even?" said Kalan in a low voice. *"No!* It cannot be this way. We cannot lose any—"

"You are losing nothing. You had nothing to lose," Kirk pointed out.

"Don't listen to this alien, Captain," urged Kislath. "Order an immediate barrage from the *Terror* and reduce his ship to rubble. Let's enjoy seeing him and all those intruders turned into cosmic dust."

"I doubt the commander of a Klingon vessel needs to be told what is the proper course of action," said McCoy, seeing Kalan's reaction to Kislath's suggestion.

The Klingon commander turned angrily on his first officer and barked, "Release them. All of them!"

"Yes, Commander," said the Klingon, obviously displeased with the way his captain ostensibly caved in to the aliens.

"We won't allow simple actions such as these to be misinterpreted so easily, Kalan," said Kirk, feeling more relaxed now that he saw not only the Andorians but his crew members coming out of the Klingon enclosure. "A channel for improved communication should be established. We can cooperate, to mutual advantage."

"Cooperate?" sneered Kalan. "Impossible. Klingons are aggressive, while other forms of life, such as yourselves, are weaklings. We will crush you."

"Whatever you say," said Kirk tiredly. "Just do it from some distance off. Is that mountain pass five kilometers to the north acceptable to you for your diggings?"

"How far?" asked the Klingon suspiciously. His other aide came and cupped a hand around a tricorder readout. Kirk decided they were studying a map display on the readout.

"Five kilometers. More if you prefer."

"Four. And not due north but rather more toward that peak." The Klingon pointed, glanced back at the tricorder for confirmation, changed his aim slightly and said, "There or nowhere."

"Dr. Threllvon-da, do you have any objections to the Klingons using their heavy equipment in the mountain pass?"

"None at all, if they will leave this site to us."

"Done!" cried Kalan. "And any caught inside our posted area will be executed without further notice. Be warned!" He and the aide stalked off in the direction already taken by Kislath. In a few minutes, the heavy machinery had been shut down and was being redirected toward the mountain area agreed upon.

"That's strange, Jim," said McCoy. "Why do you suppose they agreed so quickly to a move? Think they know something we don't?"

"I'm sure they do, Bones. Ensign Chekov, observations."

"None, sir. I make nothing out of the Klingon's behavior. This area is as nice as the mountain spot."

"I wonder," mused Kirk. "Is it really, for their purposes?"

"Whatever those clandestine purposes might be," said McCoy.

"We can be certain that they couldn't care less about archaeological knowledge," Kirk said, thinking out loud. "The idea of finding some advanced machine usable as a weapon is farfetched. Such a weapon would require energy and, after all these thousands of years, would be drained."

"Unless they sought an energy source," said Chekov.

"True, Ensign, but doubtful. The matter-antimatter reaction is as close to total annihilation and complete release of energy as we can theoretically obtain. No, I doubt the Klingons wanted anything in the site for its theoretical value to their war efforts. The Klingons are pragmatic. Whatever they wanted is obvious, except we've failed to see it."

"Looking at Threllvon-da's enthusiasm for only one thing, perhaps the Klingons just wanted to be the spoilers."

"That won't wash, Bones. They'd've destroyed the planet, not attempted to slip in. Let me check with Spock and see if he has any further information."

"Only if it's logical," scoffed McCoy.

"Spock," said Kirk, lifting his communicator, "have you been following all this?"

"Yes, Captain. I have also been following a line of inquiry which should have occurred to me earlier. Heavy equipment implies the need to move a considerable mass."

"How astute," said McCoy disdainfully. "Next you'll be telling us that the Klingons have nothing but peaceful mining in mind."

"That, Doctor, is precisely what I mean. Analysis of this planet's crustal deposits remains spotty. The geological probes of the original explorers left much to be desired. They did not indicate the extensive topaline deposits."

"Topaline!" exclamed Chekov. "That is the material used in life-support systems. It is valuable!"

"But not so valuable to us, Ensign. Not with mines on Rhyl and Talir and Spica IX. And those are only the largest deposits. We have mines on a hundred other worlds. The Federation has all the topaline it needs."

"But apparently the Klingon Empire is not so well supplied with this commodity," finished Spock.

"That explains much of their furtive behavior. Heavy mining operations aren't easily concealed. They used the guise of archaeology to bring in their diggers." Kirk walked away from the small group and stared at the Klingon encampment. They bustled around, more reminiscent of ants in their hill than individually sentient beings. He gazed around this fair world, wondering what would become of it now.

The Klingons would rape it of the topaline and any other mineral found here they happened to need. He'd seen it on dozens of worlds, and not only the Klingons were guilty. Core-deep furrows blasted into the crust of planets sucked out vital ores. Once-breathable atmospheres were contaminated with exhaust fumes, refinery fumes, coal dusts, by-products. Somehow, the concept of manufacturing and smelting in space had never caught on. The gravity afforded by a planet, plus the substance and familiarity of the surroundings for workers all prevented it—that and the abundance of rich, uninhabited worlds. Why depend on asteroids and other planetoids when entire planets could be plundered, planets that didn't require the manufacture of oxygen or water or gravity? If the ore smelted was valuable enough, lifting it out of a planet's gravity well added only a small fraction to its cost.

Kirk hated to see this pleasant world go the way of so many others. Earth itself had barely escaped such a dismal fate in the twenty-first century by reaching out into space. It was now a garden, much like this world except for the teeming billions on its surface.

"I have scanned the area you offered the Klingons in exchange for the currently mined land. The topaline concentration in the rock there is vastly higher. Indications point to the Klingon's poor instrumentation as a reason for not exploiting that area first. The configuration of the mountain range blocked their primitive probes. Actual discovery of the area probably did not occur until they were on the planet's surface and beginning their operations, at which time they established the fiction of archaeological interest and could not easily move."

"You've discovered the topaline, Spock. Have you any further information about the, uh, the force field mentioned earlier?" Kirk hesitated to mention the morale problems with his crew. While the Klingon electronics might be primitive by Federation standards, they weren't that unsophisticated. He didn't want to give Kalan any leverage at all in future dealings, not when he had been able to win every single round so far.

"Negative, Captain. I am at a loss to explain the failure. I am now exploring the possibility of neural disruption of areas in the right hemisphere of the brain."

"The part that 'erases' memory by scrambling it up like a dozen eggs?" asked McCoy. "That's a neurochemical change, not one induced by a force field."

"Any possible explanation must be examined, Doctor. If we allow even one potential source to go unnoticed, this would be most unscientific."

"Any luck?" interrupted Kirk.

"It appears that Dr. McCoy is correct. Such a field

does not exist. I have rechecked all known fields capable of affecting human metabolism and found none eliciting such varied responses. This is peculiar to Alnath II."

"I was afraid of that, Spock. Carry on. I want to look around the surface a bit more and then we'll beam back. I—"

"Captain, look!" shouted Chekov.

Kirk saw one after another of the heavy-duty mining machines of the Klingons vanish into the ground as if they were small metal insects instead of the megagram monsters they actually were.

Chapter Eight

Captain's Log: Stardate 4736.9

The Klingons accepted the new location for their topaline mining operation with alacrity. However, the sudden disappearance of their equipment—seemingly swallowed by the very planet itself—has precipitated an emergency. The *Terror's* main phaser banks have begun to glow a vivid blue from corona discharges, indicating a readiness for attack. I have ordered the crew of the *Enterprise* to general quarters. I fear attack is imminent and unavoidable.

"I've never seen anything like it before," gasped McCoy. "The whole damn planet gobbled up the Klingon machinery."

"Do you think it was sabotage?" asked Kirk of Chekov. The ensign checked and rechecked his tricorder readings.

"Unknown, Captain. My tricorder is jumbled up. Readings are all off scale. They come back now. I don't understand."

"Nor I, Ensign, nor do I," said Kirk, staring at the gaping pit where the Klingon mining machinery had growled and ripped and torn at the surface. He had the eerie feeling that *hubris* on the part of the Klingons was responsible. But that was ridiculous. He couldn't attribute godlike powers to a planet. This world wasn't alive, living, breathing, feeling. It had been deserted by its only sentient race thousands of years ago.

"Breakthrough!" came the loud cry from the Andorian compound. Threllvon-da raced out, waving his arms wildly above his head. "Breakthrough. We've finally gotten through the vault of the ceiling. And they smashed everything, just as I knew they'd do."

"Spock," said Kirk into his communicator, "verify. Did the Klingons break the roof of the subterranean city?"

"Affirmative, Captain. Every indication shows the mass of the machines exceeded the rupture point of the roof. I have obtained life-form readings through the hole. All the Klingons still live."

"But no other sentient life readings?"

"No life-form readings at all, Captain, save for the Klingons."

"Thank you, Spock." He flipped shut the lid of his communicator and turned to McCoy. Let's get down there and see if they need us, you especially. Those crewmen might be pretty banged up."

"Me?" asked McCoy in astonishment. "Me patch up a Klingon? That's not in the code, Jim."

"Aren't you dedicated to healing, no matter what life-form is injured? They need you, Bones."

"But they're Klingons."

"They're sentient beings who are injured. I can't order you to help them, but I'm asking." Kirk watched the play of emotions cross the doctor's face. He fought the dilemma quietly, then came to a decision.

"All right, Captain. But don't expect me to do much good. The Klingons have an internal structure even more scrambled up than Spock's."

Kirk smiled and set off at a brisk pace toward the gaping hole in the planetary crust. Threllvon-da and the others had preceded him. By the time Kirk, Chekov and McCoy reached the lip of the hole, the Andorian scientist had rigged a rope and was being lowered over the edge.

"Lt. Avitts," snapped Kirk, "report."

"Aye, aye, sir. The Klingons dug too deep and broke through. Then everything crashed down into Threllvon-da's city. He's fit to be tied. He's sure they've damaged valuable archaeological evidence relating to the demise of this planet's intelligent race."

"Are the Klingons hurt badly?" asked McCoy, all doctor now. "I've got my medical tricorder and a few drugs, but that's all. I can have the full kit beamed down if it's needed."

"That will be unnecessary," came Kalan's cold voice. "My men survive. Excellent equipment protected them. A few minor broken bones, nothing more. We are able to handle it."

"You're welcome," said McCoy sarcastically, noting the Klingon didn't bother to even thank him for the offer of aid.

"Why'd this happen?" burst out Chekov. "Didn't you take seismic readings of the area?"

"Our seismic readings showed nothing but solid rock. How this cavern came to be is a mystery." Kalan paced the edge of the opening glaring down into the pit, as if his scowl could lift the machinery cast down so precipitously.

"The Andorians caused this." accused Kislath bitterly. "That was the true purpose of them sneaking into our camp. They planted antimatter bombs and detonated them just as our machines passed above."

"An interesting theory, Lt. Kislath," said Kirk dryly, "but one that does not closely adhere to the facts. Dr. Threllvon-da has theorized the presence of this underground city since touching down on the planet. You were careless and just happened through the roof of that city."

"Impossible. I took the seismic readings personally. Only a fool could be deceived into believing the ground solid when a cavern actually existed. This pit was blasted by the Andorians, a clear violation of the Organian Peace Treaty. This is an act of war!"

"Will you muzzle your war dog, Captain?" growled Kirk. "His accusations are obviously wrong. He botched the readings and is trying to cover his own personal mistakes."

"What causes you to say that, Kirk?"

"Look." Kirk pointed into the blackness of the deep pit. One of the Klingon digging machines had turned on its huge spotlight. The brilliant beam smashed through the darkness and illuminated a city spun of diamond spiderwebs. Delicate flying arches supported buildings of impossible architecture. Once his eyes had adapted to the dim lighting, Kirk discerned jewels glowing with their own inner light, illuminating the streets made from a soft-appearing substance. The immensity of the city stunned him. All of this and underground exactly as Threllvon-da had predicted.

"The riches," whispered Kislath, holding his tricorder in front of him. "There are substances within the city of immense value. Topaline is used as foundation material. The diamonds of the support columns are flawless. This must be ours!"

"Yes," said Kalan, only slightly louder. "And it will be. Plundering this city will heap honor upon us. Down, get those diggers to work on the city!"

"Wait!" cried Kirk, horrified at the idea of the monstrous rock-chewing machines being turned loose in such a fragile-appearing city. "This is a scientific matter, not one of monetary importance. No amount of wealth could reimburse us if we don't learn of the civilization that constructed this city."

"We care nothing for that. They are dead. That means they were weaklings. Klingons are strong; we survive. We care nothing for the past, except our glories, our victories, our many conquests."

"We approach life somewhat differently," Kirk said cautiously. "Look at the reverence with which Threllvon-da studies the buildings. He isn't plundering. Rather, he studies. You want the topaline. Take it, but leave the city for us."

"He attempts to trick you, Captain," hissed Kislath. "He knows of our need for topaline."

"You were transparent about it," said Kirk. "But we're not trying to trick you. We want to examine the city. That's our only interest in this planet. But we need it intact for a full study. If it's looted, we will be unable to piece together important details."

"He lies, Captain. Look!" Kislath pointed to the far side of the pit. The Andorian scientists, the crew from the *Enterprise* and a group of Klingons fought a silent, fierce hand-to-hand battle. Kislath's phaser slid easily into the palm of his hand, the blunted muzzle aimed directly at Kirk's midriff.

Kislath's thumb closed on the firing contact just as Chekov struck the Klingon officer's wrist with the edge of his hand. He quickly followed the blow with a short jab to the chin. Kislath looked surprised, then slumped to the ground, knocked out by the punch. Chekov drew his own phaser and aimed it at Kalan.

"He is our prisoner now, Captain. Do you wish me to kill him?"

"Chekov, no! Remember . . . remember what happened aboard the ship. No, we don't want to harm him. We are peaceful."

"Peaceful, pah!" snorted Kalan. "Tell that to my first officer."

"He attacked me. Chekov only defended a superior officer. But let's discuss this matter after we've stopped the fighting." Kirk flipped open his communicator and barked out orders. "Lt. Avitts, halt the fighting immediately. Do it! Restrain the Andorians if necessary, but stop the fighting."

In less than a minute, the Klingons surrounded the smaller Federation party, ready to cast them into the pit. Kalan bellowed his command across the emptiness, not bothering with his communicator.

"Free them! Return to your duty posts. Get those machines out of the hole!" To Kirk, the Klingon said, "I will use the tractor beams from the *Terror*. Attempt to stop me and it will mean war!"

"Don't worry, Kalan, I won't stop you. Just leave as much of the city intact as possible when you get your diggers out."

The Klingon captain spun and marched off, leaving Kislath on the ground unconscious. Kirk glanced at the fallen officer debating whether or not to leave him to Chekov, then decided against it.

"Let's see what the city has to offer. Leave him," Kirk said, indicating Kislath. He glanced into the pit, felt a moment of passing vertigo, then thumbed open his communicator and ordered, "Spock, beam us down to the floor of this city."

The trio turned into scintillant energy, wavered and reappeared fifty meters below ground level, the magnificent city stretching as far as the eye could see.

"I've never seen anything like it," exclaimed Lt. Avitts, excited. "It's stupendous! Look at the delicate lines of the buildings. I've never even heard of a culture who built such fragile beauty into its architecture."

"I'm sure Threllvon-da knows if this fits any other culture. But I suspect it doesn't," Kirk said, awed in spite of himself. He walked to one of the walls and pressed his hand against it. A tingling sensation raced along his arm and filled his body. He tensed and started to pull away, but the soothing qualities of that contact made him keep his hand flush with the surface.

"Nice, isn't it, Captain?" asked Candra Avitts. "I don't know what it is. I had a doll when I was a small child, a soft, fluffy animal that I'd cuddle. The walls give me the same feeling."

"Ummm, yes, Lieutenant. The sensation is unique," said Kirk, reluctantly pulling away from the wall. The sense of well-being that pervaded his soul made him wonder about the builders of this city. Was this material so common they constructed entire cities from it? A single kilogram of it could command a fortune on any planet of the Federation. People would line up for hours just to experience the calmative quality.

"Stroke the road, Captain. See how you feel then," said the excited woman. She knelt down and ran her hands over the velvety roadbed. Her eyes closed and her entire body shivered as if she had some high fever. But the expression on her face told that it was no high temperature but stark ecstasy she felt.

Chekov rubbed his hands on the road and said, "Captain, it is most . . . sensual. I cannot describe this."

"Nor I, Ensign. I'm at a loss for explanation right now. This city hardly seems possible. Why should any race build itself a city with qualities such as we are experiencing?"

"One devoted to the pleasures of the flesh," suggested Lt. Avitts, continuing to stroke the road material.

"I doubt it. Did they wallow in the middle of the road? Or is that a road at all? No, Lieutenant, this city is all wrong. It has none of the lived-in feeling a real city has. It's a showcase, a perfect jewel in a diadem not intended for wear."

"It's been deserted for many thousands of years, Captain," pointed out Chekov. "We cannot expect it to be like other cities we know. This is a major find, one that will bring Threllvon-da much honor."

"It's as if the city were custom-made for the good doctor," mused Kirk. "But it's too immense. It goes on for kilometers in all directions. Is there any estimate of its size, Ensign?"

Chekov glanced at his tricorder and scowled. "My tricorder is not functioning, Captain. The readings are all wrong. Must be something in the walls of the buildings."

"My tricorder isn't working either," said Avitts. "That's odd. I just ran a diagnostic check to make certain it wouldn't go out on me again."

"Again, Lieutenant? When did it go out before?"

"Right after I landed on Alnath. Threllvon-da had begun explaining his theories about the city's existence. I turned the tricorder on to verify his idea that the Klingons were immediately above a cavern. The readings went off scale. I dismantled the tricorder, checked it and rebuilt it. The reading showing this cavern was plain then."

"How strange," said Kirk. "Where is Threllvon-da? I want to talk to him." Kirk set off at a brisk pace along the roadway, finding his distance-devouring stride actually built up his energy rather than tired him. A spring came to his step that sent surplus energy from the road up into his tired legs. The softness cushioned his feet and relaxed them. The harder he worked to tire himself, the more energy that flowed into his body from the material under his boot soles.

"Ah, Kirk, there you are. Isn't this city everything I said it would be?" crowed Threllvon-da. Kirk nodded slowly in assent. "Yes, yes, it is a marvelous city. My reputation has been great before. Now I will be the most renowned archaeologist in all the galaxy! A generation—more!—of study will be required to fully appreciate the race that constructed this magnificent metropolis."

"Is there anything in the city you didn't intend to find, Doctor?" asked Kirk. "It seems so mind-stunningly complex for a city buried and lost for several thousand years."

"They were advanced, this race was. Genius flowed in everything they did. The pyramid hinted at construction like this. The material, now, that's unique in all the galaxy. I can hardly wait to get some of my colleagues from the university here. I can use metallurgists and chemists and the finest materials scientists. Will they be fascinated! A treasure trove, Captain Kirk, a veritable storehouse of information that will furnish me with a thousand papers in the most prestigious of scientific journals."

The Andorian wandered off, muttering to himself, his tricorder storing every detailed observation, every conjecture, every hint regarding the once mighty race that had constructed this subterranean city.

Kirk shook his head. Trying to talk with the scientist was like trying to scoop space with his bare hands. The harder he worked, the less he felt he accomplished. He turned and sought his two officers. Neither Chekov nor Avitts was in sight.

"Lieutenant! Ensign!" he called out. The sound inside the city died quickly, muffled by the strange substance used in the walls. If anything, the lack of sound was the most alien feature of the city. Even in space, aboard the *Enterprise,* he heard minute sounds. The metal hull of the starship was a meter thick, but it creaked slightly due to uneven heating when near a sun. The constant motion of the crew produced sounds to reassure him that all was well. The electronics devices aboard his ship squealed and whined and whistled and rang, all at his command.

In the underground city, no sound reached his ears.

"Chekov! Avitts!" he cried again. "Where are you? Report!"

Kirk saw a blurred motion out of the corner of his eye. He spun and faced it. Nothing. No sound. No motion. Nothing. He pulled his phaser from his belt and cautiously advanced on the spot where he thought he'd seen the movement. No indication of life existed, but he sniffed deeply of the air for spoor. A lingering odor reminiscent of inefficient air-recycling dilated his nostrils.

"Klingons," he muttered.

And then all hell broke loose.

A heavy body landed squarely on his shoulders and carried him to the soft pavement. Kirk instinctively doubled up and turned his shoulder into the direction of his fall. He tucked his head under and rolled, robbing the landing of most of its shock. Like an Earth cat, he came to his feet, knees bent and the phaser held in front of him.

The Klingon who'd jumped him hadn't recovered from the attack quite as fast. He struggled to get to his knees and fumbled to pull his ray gun free from its holster. Kirk didn't give the Klingon time to level the deadly energy weapon. His phaser sang, bathed the alien in shimmering magenta, then clicked off after the predetermined duration of fire. The Klingon sank to the ground, stunned.

A sizzling blast of energy burned away hair on the side of Kirk's head. He dived again, moving, presenting as little a target to his attacker as possible. He sprawled on his belly, the pitiful hand phaser hardly a match for the more powerful and deadly ray guns used against him.

"Captain!" shouted Chekov. "To your right!"

Kirk swung around and fired. The phaser beam licked across another Klingon, dropping him unconscious in his tracks. But the one with the ray gun continued to fire. The velvety surface of the road smoldered and burned with a sickening stench. The thick black clouds from where it burned provided Kirk with enough cover to race for the position held by Chekov. He dived, his body level with the ground, and landed heavily. The air gusted from his lungs, but he had the time to suck the oxygen back into his maltreated body. Chekov stood over him, the ensign's hand phaser firing in precise bursts.

"What the hell happened?" Kirk demanded. "I left you alone for five minutes and you start a war."

"No, Captain, not us. Lt. Avitts began examining a building. She scraped off some material and performed analysis on it when Klingons came. We thought nothing of their presence until Kislath ordered them to kill us."

"Kislath!"

"Yes, Captain. He carried a portable rack of ray guns and passed them out to his crew. He said something like, 'No more orders from a miserable coward. We do things right now.' "

"Mutiny again. Kalan is going to have his hands full with Kislath, if Kislath hasn't already killed to gain control of the *Terror*."

"Would a Klingon crew follow the man who had just murdered their captain?" Chekov asked, stunned at the prospect.

"They would. They relish conflict. Promotions are as often done by assassination as by merit. In their eyes, a clever assassination is a mark of merit. One and the same. I'm glad it's not that way in the Federation Starfleet."

"So am I!" exclaimed Chekov. He ducked as another ray blast ionized a trail millimeters above his head.

"We can't stay here much longer," Kirk said. "They'll have us in a cross fire if they can get to the top of that building. With only a hand phaser, we can't outgun them, either. Let's split up and get them firing in two directions, before they do that to us. Chekov, Avitts, head toward that emerald green building. Set up a steady barrage so I can get down the street to the dull blue one. Ready, *go!*"

Kirk leaned around the low wall and began triggering his phaser in one-second bursts. The lambent energy danced off the buildings around the Klingons and forced them under cover. This allowed Chekov and Avitts to reach the shelter of the shining green structure. When they opened fire, Kirk crouched low and duck-walked, then ran all out for the other building. The street buckled under his feet from a too-close ray gun blast, but this speeded his flight. He stumbled the last few meters and landed flat on his belly, out of breath.

But his plan looked as if it was working. Avitts stunned one of the Klingons and, as another one moved to take a shot at her, Kirk lanced him with a phaser bolt. As the Klingons turned to meet this new danger, Chekov found target after target. Even with their superior arms, the Klingons had been outmaneuvered.

Kirk saw Kislath motioning for his men to regroup. This was the last thing Kirk wanted. If they could be driven out of hiding, all of them could be gunned down. He set his phaser on "detonate," took a deep breath, then heaved it like a hand grenade. It skittered across the soft pavement and bounced off the side of the building.

The explosion rocked the entire city. The Klingons were flung out by the giant fist of the blast, stumbling, dazed, unsure of their orientation. Avitts and Chekov made quick work of them.

Kirk lifted his communicator and buzzed Chekov. "Ensign, are all the Klingons accounted for?"

"Unknown, Captain. The Lieutenant and I counted nine. Normal Klingon squads number twelve. With Kislath, that's thirteen. As many as four are still loose."

Kirk cursed under his breath. It didn't take a genius to figure out he was now the weak link in the chain. Federation officers carried only a single phaser—and his had been expended in one fiery blast.

"I'll try to rejoin you. And establish contact with the *Enterprise*, if you can; let Spock know what's happening down here."

"Captain," came Avitts' clear voice, "I've tried. The ceiling of the city prevents outside contact. I'm attempting to find one of Threllvon-da's men and relay out a message."

"Good," he said. "I'll be with you shortly."

He replaced his communicator and surveyed the scene. The carnage wrought by his overload phaser attack struck him as totally incongruous. The blackened walls, the ripped apart street, the scattered bodies of the Klingons were totally out of place in this perfectly manicured city. He shook his head in wonder. The ancient metropolis was maintained better than most living, breathing, populated cities.

Squinting, trying to detect any indication of the remaining four Klingons, Kirk witnessed something that made a cold lump form in the pit of his stomach. The walls of the building, once blistered and discolored from the phaser blast, slowly repaired themselves. Like a living being, the city mended itself. In less than a minute, the wall had returned to its pristine condition. Even the cavity blasted into the street had started to fill in, fixed as no human crew could ever accomplish in such a short time.

"The whole damned place is alive," he muttered. "I wonder what it thinks about our shooting holes in it."

He sprinted for the cover of the next building and the next and the next. He peered around a corner and waited. No sound reached his ears. Kirk rose and started to race for the protection of still another building when he smelled the telltale odor of a Klingon. Kirk froze, then relaxed, his muscles ready for instant action.

He moved a fraction of a second before the butt of a ray gun would have smashed his skull. He caught the blow on his shoulder. Pain seared along his nerves but he ignored it. The man grappled with his Klingon adversary. Caught off balance, the alien staggered backward. Kirk's leg shot out in a circular sweeping action and pulled the Klingon's legs out from under him. They landed heavily, Kirk's elbows positioned directly over the Klingon's stomach. The sound of air gushing from tortured lungs almost deafened Kirk. He punched a short, hard blow into an exposed chin, and the Klingon lay limp, knocked out.

Kirk hefted the fallen ray gun, noting the unfamiliar feel. The powerful weapon could raze half this city, even if the city regenerated itself. The sound of two Klingons angrily whispering warned Kirk. He spun, fired from instinct and burned a hole through the corner of a nearby building. The shock wave from the blast knocked down both Klingons.

"Don't reach for your phasers," he warned them. Kirk pulled out his communicator and flipped it open. "Avitts, Chekov, I have the last of the Klingons. Home in on my signal. Kirk out." He placed the activated communicator at his feet. His eyes never left the two aliens sprawled on the ground.

A crunching noise caused by a heavy boot sole smashing his communicator caused Kirk to break concentration. He looked down the barrel of a heavy ray gun held competently in Kislath's hand.

"I won't shoot, Kirk. Not yet. I want the other two, also."

"We can negotiate," said Kirk, his mouth suddenly dry. "Put your gun away and I'll let these two go."

"You use them as hostages? Hardly, Kirk," sneered Kislath. "They mean nothing to me. If you kill them, all your leverage over me is gone. And if you are too weak to shoot, then you pose no threat at all to them. Either way, you are dead, space scum."

Kirk was looking straight into Kislath's cold eyes when he saw the Klingon stiffen, surprise masking his features. Kislath folded like an accordion, his dropped ray gun clacking dully on the pavement.

"Lt. Kislath exceeded his authority," said Kalan in measured tones. The Klingon captain held a phaser in his hand. His thumb worked restlessly on the trigger, as if he debated about repeatedly stunning his fallen officer. Several quick bursts of even the sunning ray would paralyze the heart, killing Kislath.

"I'm glad you think so," breathed Kirk heavily. He straightened, but the ray gun barrel never deviated from the line of fire at the Klingon.

"That ray gun won't be required, Kirk."

"It's yours, anyway," Kirk said, tossing it to Kalan. The Klingon fielded it easily and tucked it into his belt. "My two officers will be here in a few minutes. Don't get too nervous with your phaser."

"No," said Kalan, returning it to his belt. "This attack was unprovoked. I monitored it and came as soon as I could. A squad loyal to me is picking up *his* men. They will be disciplined severely."

"Executed?"

"Perhaps. Perhaps I will interrogate Kislath first. That would give me great pleasure. This upstart is after honor and fame at my expense. I cannot allow that. It constitutes mutiny."

"Such as you've already had," probed Kirk, wanting to keep the Klingon commander uneasy.

"Such is the life of any in the Space Service of the Empire. I survive. I am the fittest, the strongest, the smartest, the quickest. When I fail, another will take my place better suited to command. But it will not be *him*." The distaste in Kalan's voice rang out loud and clear. "He is the spawn of a first secretary and thinks he is destined for my position—and more. Oh, yes, this gives me great pleasure."

Kalan glanced up as Avitts and Chekov ran up, phasers in hand. Kirk motioned for them to hold their fire.

"Thank you, Captain. You saved me from having a hole drilled through my head by your first officer."

"I did you no favors. If I hadn't wanted him for my own reasons, I would have cheered him on." With that, Kalan turned and stalked off, head held arrogantly high.

"Three to beam up," Kirk said into the borrowed communicator. Kirk, Avitts and Chekov shimmered, then vanished from the face of Alnath II, to be reconstructed in the transporter room of the *Enterprise*.

"I'm glad to see you, Jim," said McCoy worriedly. "That machine is acting up again. Getting so the thing's more a menace than an aid, if it ever was that."

"I'm glad to be back, too, Bones. But for different reasons. That transporter is one of the few things left in the universe I can rely on." He glanced at Lt. Kyle and wondered how truthful his statement really was. The transporter chief idly ran his fingers over a clay bust, forming and shaping his work rather than attending to the complex functioning of the transporter.

"Lt. Kyle," Kirk asked mildly, "are you on duty?"

"Yes, sir," he said, not paying that much attention to his commanding officer.

"Do you remember what I mentioned would happen to you if I caught you being the least bit inattentive to your post—after the first dereliction of duty?"

"Uh, yes, sir, I do. But not to worry. I'm watching everything closely. Isn't it nice, sir?" he asked, pointing to his clay sculpture. "But there's something not quite right with the nose. Perhaps a little more clay to lengthen it. What do you think, sir?"

"Carry on, Mr. Kyle. And Bones, I'm happy the transporter worked right, too." Kirk and the others quickly went to the wardroom where the senior officers had already assembled. Spock called them to attention.

Kirk eyed his first officer, noting the unmistakable tensing of the facial muscles when Spock saw Candra Avitts. The Vulcan fought down his emotionalism and said, "Welcome aboard, Captain."

"Thank you, Mr. Spock. Please be seated, all of you." Kirk remained on his feet, studying them. Some paid him rapt attention while others obviously wished to be elsewhere following their own pursuits. Kirk noted that there was no correlation between those he considered to be the most capable in their posts and their current attention—or inattention. Scotty nervously shifted back and forth in his chair, as if the seat had been electrically wired and gave him constant shocks. Kirk guessed his chief engineer wanted to return to the engine room and squeeze another few ergs from the warp drive.

"Lt. Avitts, report on the city," ordered Kirk. He sat and leaned back in his chair. He listened with only half a mind; the other half turned over factors, put them together, tested them and pulled them apart in a vain attempt to get to the bottom of the mystery facing the *Enterprise.*

The woman reported concisely, accurately and in detail. She left out nothing of importance and included a myriad details of inconsequence, realizing that none of them knew what might give the vital clue.

"Thank you, Lieutenant. As you have just heard, this city Threllvon-da has discovered is unique. Mr. Spock, has anything like it ever been discovered on any other planet?"

"Negative, Captain. However, Threllvon-da wrote a research paper several years ago on the possibility of a culture building a city similar to this. Certain details vary, but it is essentially the one outlined in the report."

"Self-repairing, sensuous, silent, all those were included?" Kirk asked.

"Yes, Captain, all those. But the brilliant colors of the actual buildings were not mentioned at that time nor was the spiderweb construction. There is some indication that the buttressing used is purely ornamental. From Lt. Avitts' tricorder readings," Spock said, his voice catching so slightly only Kirk noticed it, "the buildings themselves are more than adequately strong to support their mass. They are constructed of a Canfield-type piezoelectric material, weak until an appropriate electrical current is run through it. It then becomes stronger than steel until the current is turned off. This is a fascinating application of an effect long known to our science."

"So those buildings have a continuous electric charge running through them?" asked Kirk, intrigued.

"Put crudely, yes," replied Spock.

"Where does the power come from? After thousands of years, any generator known to our science would have broken down."

"Unknown, Captain," admitted Spock.

"Then it's possible that whatever supplies the energy for the buildings might also supply the power for the force field acting upon us?"

"Possible, but unlikely. I have conducted a painstaking search and have discovered nothing. It is as if the energy used by the city is being created from . . . nothing."

"Impossible," scoffed McCoy. "You can't get something for nothing. That's one of the laws of thermodynamics."

"Unscientifically stated, but yes, Doctor, that is true."

"You're admitting, then, that you know nothing about what is down there on the planet?" demanded McCoy.

"You know that already. I have scrutinized Alnath and discovered less than Threllvon-da. How he has managed to do so much in such a short time is nothing less than a tribute to his genius."

"Miracles, Spock? I didn't think you believed in them. Aren't they just like luck?" taunted McCoy. Kirk settled in his chair and tented his fingers in front of his lips, watching the byplay between his two friends. He knew he should stop it, yet something inside kept him silent.

"I don't believe in anything that cannot be scientifically verified through experimentation. Some aspects of science are of dubious nature but must be accepted because they present the simplest possible explanation. I hold them to be workable theories until other, newer, more comprehensive ones are formulated."

"Try this one on for size," said McCoy. "This still-unknown force acts outward from the core of the planet. It affects humans, Andorians, Klingons and Vulcans in different ways due to differences in their physiologies. We humans tend toward whimsical pursuits, the Andorians become absorbed in their work, Klingons become more aggressive and Vulcans," McCoy said, pausing dramatically, "Vulcans are killed by this force."

"An interesting speculation, Dr. McCoy," said Spock in a cool, level voice. "But it fails to take into account my continued existence. I feel fit. This mysterious field of yours has not harmed me."

"That's because you're a half-breed, Spock. You're neither fish nor fowl. You're in between. You're what happened when the horse snuck into the donkey's stall."

"Enough, Doctor," said Kirk briskly. "We are not here to provide an in-depth analysis by way of analogy to Mr. Spock's genes. There appear to be more questions raised by your conjecture than are answered. What *exactly* happened to the Vulcans? Remember the situation. No marks of physical violence, the autopsies revealed no malfunctioning of any vital organs, no dearth of enzymes or amino acids or other bodily chemicals. They simply . . . died."

McCoy shrugged and sat back. "All I was saying is that being a half-breed probably saved Spock from the same fate. Nothing else."

Kirk watched Spock straining, fighting to hold back a retort. This anger was unlike the Vulcan. The emotional, human side of the man boiled to the surface again, raging at the racial slurs heaped upon him by McCoy. Spock gripped the edge of the table so hard that Kirk wondered if his powerful grip might actually leave fingerprints in the surface. As he watched, Kirk saw Mr. Spock relax by force of his own will.

"I will consider your comments, Dr. McCoy," Spock said in a calm voice. Of all those at the table, only Kirk realized the effort Spock put into sounding at ease.

"Very well. We'll go from department to department checking on the status of the *Enterprise*. Mr. Scott, the engines are—"

"Battle stations!" blared the intercom. "Battle stations! The Klingons are firing on us!"

Kirk raced for the turbo-elevator, his heart in his throat and adrenaline pumping.

Chapter Nine

Captain's Log: Stardate 4737.1

> The *Enterprise* has sustained minor damage from the Klingon attack. Deflector screens are holding; phaser banks are fully charged, waiting for my command to attack. Although the attack was unprovoked, I am hesitant to return fire. The Organian Peace Treaty must be preserved at all costs or the resulting interstellar war will devastate uncountable planets. The Klingons must be stopped here at Alnath II—peacefully.

"Status report, Mr. Sulu," Kirk demanded as he made his way to the command seat. Never before had that throne seemed so high and imposing to him. He and he alone dictated the course of the next few minutes. A proper decision meant safety for the *Enterprise* and its crew. A mistake meant death.

And war.

"Klingons are increasing the attack, sir," said the helmsman. "I have ordered the screens to full deflection, but they're weakening."

"Engineering, report."

"Aye, Captain," came Scott's voice. "We're puttin' in as much power as we can to the screens. The radiation level's risin', risin' much too fast."

"Estimates, Scotty."

"We canna survive more'n ten minutes at this rate, Cap'n!"

Kirk flicked off the intercom and stared at the viewscreen. The sight of the Klingon vessel firing its phaser batteries angered him. He wanted to lash out, to return fire, to test the potency of the *Enterprise*'s weapons against the massiveness of the *Terror*.

What was it Kalan had said? That it would be an interesting test to pit a heavy cruiser against a dreadnought.

He slammed his fist against the armrest of the command seat. He couldn't fight. He dare not open fire. The *Enterprise* might outmaneuver the Klingon ship but it couldn't outrun or outfight it. The limitations of his hardware made that apparent.

"Captain, awaiting your order to fire," Sulu said, anxiously. His finger poised over the phaser trigger button.

"Don't, Mr. Sulu, not yet. Mr. Spock, have you analyzed the Klingon phaser beam frequency yet?"

"They have tunable phasers and have found the single frequency at which our deflector shield is weakest."

"Can we tune the screen and get away from that particular frequency? Can you give us another few minutes?"

"Certainly, Captain, but that is futile. We might as well lower the screens and allow them to destroy us." The defeat and sorrow in Spock's voice made Kirk spin around.

"Mr. Spock, we will not commit suicide."

"But, Captain, that's what you're doing!" cried Sulu. "Give the order to open fire. We may not be able to destroy them, but let's go out fighting!"

"Make them regret the day they fired on us!" came another voice. And still another on the far side of the bridge said, "Filthy Klingons don't deserve a clean phaser death. Should let them all breathe vacuum!"

"Silence!" bellowed Kirk, his face reddening. "I will not hear any such talk on my bridge. I am in command of this starship, and its safety is entrusted to me and me alone. Is that clear?"

A few grumblings came. Kirk spun around and snapped, "Mr. Sulu, you will resume your position as helmsman. Mr. Chekov, plot a course around the curvature of the planet to get us out from under the Klingons' guns. Mr. Sulu, execute the course immediately. And dammit, keep your finger off the phaser controls!"

"The screens have been retuned, Captain," came

Spock's voice. The Vulcan sounded as if he would cry at any instant. "But I fear it's a lost cause. They can retune to match our change. We're lost." Defeatism rang from his words.

"Mr. Spock, I need you," said Kirk earnestly. "Don't do this to me. Get a hold of yourself." He almost wished for the cold-bloodedly emotionless robot again. In a crisis situation such as this, that would be better than a whimpering, cowed first officer.

"Captain, you just don't understand," said Spock, his eyes filling with tears. "They're too powerful! They'll destroy us."

Kirk slapped him across the face. The stinging slap sounded like a beam breaking under stress. The Vulcan lifted his hand to his injured face, the tears obvious on his cheeks now. Kirk slapped him again.

"Get mad, Spock," he snarled. "Get mad at me. Hate me, threaten me, do something! I need you!" Kirk slapped Spock again. This produced the desired results.

Steely fingers gripped Kirk's wrist and held his hand easily just millimeters away from its target.

"Do that again and I'll break your arm."

"Good, Spock, now get mad at them! If you have to be emotional, I want you reacting with usable emotions, emotions that won't get us all killed."

Spock's lips thinned as he fought to keep from striking back, from screaming, from raging emotionally. As he watched, Kirk saw the veil of total logic slip back over the Vulcan. He eased the death grip on Kirk's wrist and nodded.

"Very well, Captain, if that is what you wish." He pivoted and went back to his computer console, busily working to find the frequencies least dangerous to the *Enterprise* from the Klingon attack.

Kirk heaved a deep sigh. He felt the entire bridge rebelling against him. Every single officer reacted differently. Spock ran the gamut of emotions before sinking into his all-too-Vulcan facade of pure logic. Chekov obviously strained to keep from repeating the same mistake he'd made earlier. Kirk nodded in approval. Chekov's hands might tremble every time they passed near the phaser firing control, but he didn't relent and disobey orders. Sulu sulked. He did his job with lackluster movements, as if reluctant to flee from the Klingons. Others on the bridge shared these sentiments.

Kirk heard one of the engineering officers mutter, "Turning tail and running. Never thought I'd see it."

"Lt. Uhura," said Kirk, sure that his officers were doing their jobs, if under duress, "open hailing frequencies to the *Terror*. I want to speak with Kalan."

"Aye, aye, sir," said the woman, the tone of her voice indicating she preferred to fight rather than talk with the Klingons.

Kirk settled back, his eyes darting around the bridge. The immediate danger had abated. The *Enterprise* had increased its orbital speed and put more of Alnath's atmosphere between it and the Klingon ship. The beam attenuation robbed the powerful phasers of their sting, at least to the point where the deflector screens handled the punishment.

"You surrender?" came the harsh tones of a Klingon.

"I'd see the person to whom I'm speaking," said Kirk stonily. The screen flowed and solidified. Kirk straightened in his seat, nodding slowly now that he understood the situation.

"Yes, Kirk. I am the new captain of the *Terror*," said Kislath. "I have disposed of the weakling who commanded this fine vessel before me. Will you surrender? It would be a great coup for the Empire to display your struck colors in our Hall of Honor."

"I hadn't intended to surrender, Kislath. Especially to an upstart like you. Let me speak with Kalan. Or some ranking officer, not a vacuum-brained coward."

"Coward?" screamed Kislath. The Klingon turned and barked an order. Kirk noticed the red lights flaring all over the *Enterprise*'s bridge. The attack had been doubled, tripled, quadrupled in ferocity. "We'll see who is the coward, Kirk. You will crawl—seconds before we turn your ship into molten liquid."

"Mr. Sulu, increase orbital speed and compensate for increased angular momentum using the artificial gravity." He felt himself being swung around by centrifugal force due to a higher speed while maintaining the same altitude above the planet. Sulu quickly balanced the forces and returned the ship to its Earth normal gravity.

"Mr. Chekov, keep the Klingon ship on the horizon. This puts the maximum amount of atmosphere between them and us while keeping them in sight. I don't want them sneaking around and coming head on at us."

"Aye, aye, sir," said Chekov, warming to the cat-and-mouse chase. "What should I tell phaser crews?"

"Maintain battle alert, nothing more. I'll have the crew member's ears on a plate if anyone fires without my order."

Spock came up and said, "The deflector screens are hooked into the computer. A Klingon phaser blast will be analyzed and the computer will appropriately alter the frequency to present the maximum possible defense."

"Very good, Spock. Write it up and we'll give it to Starfleet Command to counter future Klingon attacks."

"It was the logical outgrowth of the situation, Captain."

"Logical?" smiled Kirk. "Yes, I suppose it was. Right now, I've got to convince Kislath that he doesn't really want to blow the *Enterprise* to atoms."

"A problem with diminishing probability of solution," said Spock.

"Only if you run it through a computer, Mr. Spock. Kislath's weaknesses aren't the ones likely to mean much to a machine. And that's what I'm counting on." Kirk's mind turned over the idea forming to examine each and every facet. Finally, he said to his first officer, "Any further data obtained about the force acting on Alnath?"

"Negative, Captain. If we cannot register this force on our instruments, we cannot measure it. Therefore, we know nothing about it."

"You're wrong, Spock. Or rather, you're not watching the right instruments. I've got a good reading on one right now. Lt. Uhura, open channel to the *Terror*. Hurry."

The viewscreen flowed into the swarthy face of Kislath. He sneered as he said, "You surrender now or do you wish to hide like cowards for a short while longer?"

"I tire of dealing with subordinates. Put on a senior officer so I can talk to him."

Kirk watched the anger flare on Kislath's face. Spock said quietly, "Is it in our best interest to antagonize the Klingon? His vessel is the stronger and faster."

"I'm just taking an instrument reading, Mr. Spock," Louder, for Kislath to hear, "If one isn't available, then call your sanitation engineer. I want to order him to remove your garbage-carcass from the bridge of such a fine ship."

"I will destroy you!" screamed Kislath, pounding his fists on a table in front of him as he half-rose. "I will . . ." The sentence fell off into incoherence as he sputtered angrily.

"You tire me with your petulance. If you want to remove me, why don't we meet in a duel of honor on Alnath's surface? Assuming that a child like you has any honor, of course. Do you?"

"You challenge, I accept! Any weapons! In one hour in the underground city." Kislath's finger stabbed out and the circuit was broken.

"Do you wish me to open another hailing frequency, Captain?" asked Uhura.

"That won't be necessary. I think I got the message loud and clear. Mr. Spock, status report."

"The *Terror* has ceased firing."

"Very good. Mr. Sulu, position us directly over the Andorian camp once again. I have to prepare for a little meeting with our Klingon friend. You have the conn, Mr. Spock."

The officers on the bridge were silent as they watched their captain enter the turbo-elevator.

"Don't be a fool, Jim. That Klingon will chop you into goose liver," said McCoy angrily.

"You appear to have a low opinion of your old captain," said Kirk, smiling. "I know what I'm doing. Kislath has mutinied. If Kalan is still alive, Kislath's position may shift for the worse. If not, well, we're in no worse shape for my meeting him down on Alnath."

"We are!" shouted McCoy. "You can get yourself killed. Don't throw your life away like this. That backstabbing Klingon practices being sneaky. It's part of his way of life. You can't compete with him in a duel."

"I have to, if we want to maintain our position in the Alnath system," said Kirk, sobering. "The *Terror* is too powerful a ship. If we'd returned fire, they'd have seen that as sufficient cause to blow us out of the sky."

"They tried to do that anyway, without all these highfalutin theories of yours. You're beginning to sound like Spock."

"How is that, Doctor?" came the Vulcan's cold question. Fire burned in Spock's eyes. Kirk felt the raging anger like an open plasma torch. The Vulcan had flipped over again and operated on a purely emotional basis. He had to move to defuse this confrontation before one of his friends said or did something they would later regret.

"Mr. Spock, is all in readiness?"

"Yes, Captain. I feel we should train the ship's batteries on you in case of treachery. We can devastate the Klingon camp and all within it at an instant's notice."

"No, Spock. This is a duel. While Starfleet Command might frown on one of its captains participating, it isn't illegal. If I win, we have prevented a war. If I lose, at least the *Enterprise* is still capable of fighting."

"We need you, Jim," said McCoy earnestly. "Without you this ship is little more than a pile of nuts and bolts. You hold it together."

Kirk laughed nervously. "You overestimate my role, Bones. While the *Enterprise* isn't ranking high on the efficiency scale right now, it is the best ship with the best crew in the entire fleet. I'm the one privileged to be captain; it's not the other way around." Kirk put his hand on McCoy's shoulder and said, "Sometimes I think peace is only war in disguise. It's my duty to get us through this."

"You appear to know something that we do not, Captain," said Spock, all trace of anger gone. The cold tone of his statement told Kirk his science officer was still on the emotional seesaw. "Have you discerned the true nature of the force acting in this system?"

"Let's say I've approached the problem in a different way than you have, Spock. Instead of trying to figure out scientifically what the force is, I've accepted its existence and have tried to figure out how to use it to my advantage. I just hope my empirical approach works." He cinched up his belt, checking his phaser and communicator. "Has Threllvon-da been informed of my arrival?"

"He was disinterested, Captain," said Spock. "His full attention is on the city. Unless the sun goes nova, he couldn't care less what happens around him."

"And," added McCoy, "the only reason the sun going nova would bother him is that it would cost him his precious city."

"Just as well," Kirk said, taking a deep breath to settle his nerves. Now that the time of the duel was at hand, he began to feel jittery. He rubbed his hands together and said, "Time for me to go. You have your orders. I expect you to obey them to the letter. Do I make myself clear?"

Both men nodded, Spock curtly and McCoy reluctantly.

"Good. Beam me down." He moved to the center of one of the transporter disks and waited. The field gripped him and threw the disassembled atoms across space to rebuild him on Alnath II.

He came out of the transporter beam in a crouch, his hand resting on his phaser. Only the wind howled across the deserted plain. He pulled out his communicator and spoke softly, "Kirk to *Enterprise*. No one in sight. What do the life sensor readings say?"

"The Klingon is in the city. He transported directly underground a few minutes ahead of you," came Spock's imperturbable voice.

"I'll drop in on him using a rope. There's one nearby. Kirk out." He went and fastened one end of the rope around a nearby stake driven into the ground. He tugged on the rope to insure its security, then kicked out and slid down until he dangled a few meters above the street level. Hanging, turning slowly, Kirk used his aerial vantage point to reconnoiter.

He saw Kislath immediately. The Klingon crouched behind a low wall, ray gun in hand, waiting for Kirk to come by. This wasn't intended to be a duel; it was planned as an execution, if Kirk allowed it.

The factor Kirk had been hoping for entered the equation. Kalan still lived. The Klingon captain also moved silently through the underground city, a phaser in his hand. If Kirk played the game properly, he could set the two against each other and bide his time. He slid the rest of the way to the city street and crouched, waiting, plotting. Secure in his knowledge of Kislath's hiding place and of the course Kalan took through the city, he set off.

A major intersection provided all the space Kirk needed to prepare his trap. He dropped onto his belly and sighted along the top of his phaser at a point just centimeters above where Kalan's head would appear. The instant the black-haired head poked around the corner, Kirk fired.

And he immediately backed off, stood and ran down the street. He cut down a side street and prepared another trap. He knew now that Kalan stalked him.

"Kislath, you lover of *lorks,* I'll rip out your liver and devour it," shouted the angry Klingon. Kirk waited. "Do you hear me, Kislath? Marooning me in this city is treason. Mutiny!' '

Kirk fired again to keep the Klingon commander interested. He didn't retreat after firing, however. He had studied Klingon psychology for many hours, trying to fathom the way they thought, how they acted and reacted. Together with a computer analysis of the most likely move from Kalan, Kirk had a better than fifty-fifty chance of outguessing the Klingon.

Only a slight noise betrayed Kalan. He had spoken loudly, trying to bait the man he thought to be Kislath, then hastened to circle, sure that his quarry would attempt retreating again. Kirk retraced his path down the side street and continued toward Kislath's position. This cat-and-mouse hunting stimulated him. He pitted himself against two Klingons, not just one. The adrenaline flowed and brought him heightened awareness. For the first time in months, he truly lived. The soldier in him was allowed free expression, free action.

He enjoyed being a soldier. He had been trained as extensively for war as he had for peace; it was required of all Academy cadets. He vented his killing urges easily now that he lured Kalan into the jaws of Kislath's trap.

But this wasn't what he intended. Almost sorrowfully, he cut off the street and pressed himself flat into a peculiarly shaped doorway. He heard the cat-soft padding of Kalan's boots on the velvety material of the street.

"Kislath, you spawn of dishonored fools, do battle with me!"

Kirk fired his phaser and bounced one of the violet beams off the top of the wall behind Kislath. The Klingon believed Kalan sighted in on him.

Kislath dived from behind the wall, his ray gun purring a deadly song. The intense beam of energy darted wildly as he changed positions. Smoking, blackened sections of street and building remained as reminders of the Klingon's treachery.

Kalan never noticed Kirk's weaker hand phaser firing. He was too intent on Kislath. He darted out into the street and rested his phaser on his left forearm for steadier firing. Shot after shot dogged Kislath's heels. Finally, one of the beams connected and sent the mutineer stumbling.

Seeing this, Kirk acted. He circled to the side of the building, his back flat against the wall as he moved. The electric field soothed him, reassured him. For a moment, he forgot about his mission, then pulled away from the seductive building to see the tableau formed in the center of the street. Kislath held out his ray gun, poised to fire. Kalan held his phaser aimed directly at his first officer. Neither of them moved, as if assessing the other's probability of success.

"You're not Kirk," said Kislath finally. "Did he send you to do his killing?"

"I do my own," Kalan said hotly. "I need no Federation weakling to aid me in dispensing justice."

Kirk saw Kislath's finger tightening around the trigger of his ray gun. He fired, stunning Kislath. But the shock of the phaser beam striking him produced a convulsive jerk that caused the ray gun to fire. His shot went off target, but not by much. Kalan screamed in pain and collapsed to the street.

Kirk rushed to Kislath, kicked aside the ray gun and saw that his aim had been true. The Klingon was unconscious. Turning to Kalan, he saw a wound that sickened him. Kalan writhed in pain, a hole as large as a fist punched through his side.

"You did this, Kirk. You set us against one another," accused Kalan.

"You did it all to yourselves. I challenged him to a duel on the planet, but I didn't know you were still alive. When I found out, I only used you to prevent him from destroying the *Enterprise*."

"Your damned *Enterprise*," gasped Kalan. "But I understand." With pain wracking his features, he looked up into Kirk's eyes. Silent communication flowed. The two came as close to understanding each other as they ever would. They shared duty above all else. Then the rapport faded as Kalan doubled over in pain.

"Let me get you some medical help," Kirk offered, flipping open his communicator. "Kirk to *Enterprise*. Beam down McCoy on the double. Full alien med-kit. One of the Klingons is seriously injured." He flipped shut the lid of the communicator before any aboard the ship protested.

"I want none of your alien medicine doctors. They are all butchers."

"Many on my vessel say the same about all Klingons," said Kirk mildly. "Just relax and you'll be all right. That energy beam cauterized the wound. You're in no danger of bleeding to death."

"Shock," muttered Kalan. "systemic shock is setting in. I must . . . kill him first."

"Kislath?"

"Of course, Kislath! You fool. He marooned me in this city. I lost command of my ship because of him. He won't live to gloat. He must die. Drag me close enough so that I can strangle him with my own hands."

"You're not strong enough," Kirk said, stalling for time. He knew it would be only a few more minutes before McCoy arrived with the med-kit.

"I'll shove my phaser against his heart and fire it until he dies. I care not how he dies, as long as he *dies!*" Kalan started crawling toward the unconscious Kislath. Kirk marveled at the determination locked in the Klingon's body. The pain had to be excruciating, and yet he continued to move slowly, a few centimeters at a time, toward his enemy.

Kislath stirred, fighting the effects of Kirk's phaser.

"Kill him, *kill him!*" cried Kalan. "Promise me you will kill him if I die before I can reach him."

Kirk aimed his phaser again and the beam struck Kislath squarely in the chest. The Klingon fell heavily to the pavement, stunned again.

"Good," sighed Kalan, thinking his first officer had died. "I may go to my ancestors with honor now." He sank to the velvety pavement, a grim smile on his lips.

A shimmering column of energy appeared a few meters away. Medical help had arrived.

"I'm a doctor, not a veterinarian, Jim," stormed McCoy. "How am I supposed to piece together something that looks like that?" He pointed to the supine body of the Klingon on his operating table.

"And all this time I thought you knew everything, Bones. You're shaking my confidence in you. The next time I have a wart, I'll ask M'Benga to remove it."

"The next time you have a wart, I'll make sure the virus eats you alive," said McCoy, glaring at Kirk. "What is it you expect me to do with him?"

"I just want to get him patched up so you can ship him back to the *Terror*."

"An autopsy would be easier. He's pretty far gone. Look at the respiration. Almost zero. Heart rate is too slow. Metabolism is fouled up. Those enzymes aren't supposed to be there. I'd bet the south forty on that." McCoy peered at the readout on his operating table console, trying to figure out what should be normal and what was indicative of major injury. "This is probably okay," he said, tapping his knuckle against the left slide-indicator.

"As you say, Doctor. Do what you can."

"This is collaboration with the enemy," grumbled McCoy. "Nurse Chapel, get my instruments in here."

"Which ones, Doctor?" she asked sweetly. "The computer-driven ones or your hand-held ones?"

"My computer ones, for Pete's sake. What's wrong with you, Nurse? Can't you see that the slightest error will mean a death on my operating table? I can't risk a mistake using a museum piece."

He mumbled as he set up the sterile field over Kalan's midsection. Strong fingers probed and caused the readouts above the operating table to bounce.

"He's strong, Jim. I may be able to do something for him. Nurse, inject ten cc.s of ACTH and see if cortisone levels rise. If not, hit him with as strong a dose of cordrazine as you can get into an injector."

"Yes, Doctor."

Kirk stood back and watched them operate. McCoy fought his suspicion of all mechanical devices and relied heavily on his computer-assisted surgical tools. The man was too caught up in the surgery to notice any change in his own behavior. Kirk breathed easier when he realized that McCoy was going to save Kalan.

"This is incredible," McCoy said, digging in the cavity of Kalan's chest. "Record this, Nurse. Amygdala in chest cavity, function unknown. Aliphatic compounds being analyzed by the computer now. Mucus obstruent, cleaning with low suction. Some tissue reaction caused by epedaphic . . ."

"Dr. McCoy, are you healing him or stripping him to sell the spare parts?" asked Kirk. "I want him talking as soon as possible. The *Terror* still doesn't know we have both Kalan and Kislath aboard. I can't keep them in the dark much longer."

"I'm hurrying, I'm hurrying. But if I rush too much, I'll have to carve another notch in the leg of my operating table. Anabolic protoplaser. I'm closing now." He took the slender instrument and applied it to the wound. A buzzing sound filled the room as he slowly pulled the sides of the wound together and speeded their healing. "Too much skin lost from the ray gun to pull the wound entirely together. Bring me some plastiskin, Nurse."

A roll of the artificial skin was slapped into the doctor's hand. He pulled off a few square centimeters and covered the gaping hole in the Klingon's side. "This is against my better judgment. Might be rejection due to differences in body chemistry."

"Do it, Bones. I need him awake."

"All right. Spot welding skin. Low energy pulsed laser." Nurse Chapel wheeled the power supply closer, and McCoy concentrated on burning tiny holes in the skin and melting the plastiskin into them. In a few minutes, the once ugly hole in Kalan's chest had been closed. Only the paleness of his normally swarthy face betrayed the seriousness of his injury.

"You shouldn't talk with him for forty-eight hours," said McCoy, "but I know that a mere doctor's advice is not worth a pile of peanut shells around here. Five cc.s of benjisidrine—and some tri-ox to help his breathing. Don't keep him longer than five minutes, Jim. This isn't doctor's advice, it's common sense. He'll be very weak."

"He'll be spitting fire," declared Kirk. And he was right. In less than a minute, Kalan came out of his drug-induced coma.

"What right have you to bring me aboard your ship?" he demanded.

"I'm sorry now I fixed him up," said McCoy sardonically. "I should've performed that autopsy after all. The Stellar Medical Association would have been interested in his innards—in a glass jar. They're even weirder than Spock's."

Kirk silenced the doctor with a glance, then turned to Kalan. "You are going to be all right, at least until we can get you back to your own doctors aboard the *Terror*."

"Your concern for me is touching," Kalan sneered.

"We have mutual concerns."

The Klingon stared at Kirk for a moment, then asked, "Why didn't you return fire when Kislath attacked your ship? I'd have fought."

"We're peaceful and cannot easily be provoked into breaking the peace treaty." Kirk ignored the contemptuous snort. "As long as that treaty is in force, we are not enemies. Are you tracking that? *We are not enemies.*"

"Our aims conflict on this planet. We both want topaline. *We* shall have it."

"We don't want the ore. Our reasons for being here are as previously stated: we must defend our citizens."

"Pah!"

"The Vulcans died. Seventy-two of them. The Federation can't allow their deaths to go unexplained."

"We did not do it. We know nothing of it."

"I'm forced to believe you. The testimony of Threllvon-da and the other Andorians in his archaeological party supports that. No evidence exists that you have the technology to kill tracelessly."

"If we had such a weapon we would have used it long ago," said Kalan. "We are not ones to allow weapons technology to languish. Such advances are field tested at the earliest possible time."

"There is that warlike propensity on your part." Kirk sighed. "But we're not arguing. I don't believe you had any part in killing the Vulcans. Your actions since then have been less than peaceful, but this can be attributed to Kislath, I feel. My report to Starfleet Command will indicate that."

"Why are you doing this? You could excoriate all Klingons, yet you choose to lay blame on only one. You have the reason for a just war in your grasp. Why do you not take it?"

"No war is just, Kalan. We fight only in self-defense. If even a single Federation citizen is threatened, this is reason enough for all to join in war. But that provocation has to be great."

"Weaklings," sneered Kalan.

"You think so. We have differing philosophies of behavior. We have different goals, different ways of attaining them. But that doesn't mean we have to be adversaries. Negotiation is better for both sides rather than all-out interstellar war."

Kalan snorted loudly and lounged back on the table. "Allow me to contact my ship. I wish to transfer as quickly as possible. I do not want such weakness contaminating my mind."

Kirk nodded to McCoy, who injected a sedative into the Klingon's arm. In seconds, the tenseness faded from Kalan's face. He slept.

"Like watching a rabid dog go to sleep, isn't it?" said McCoy. "I put enough strelamine into him to keep him quiet for at least eight hours."

"Good. That gives us time." Kirk left the sick bay, his mind leaping ahead to what he must do.

Chapter Ten

Captain's Log: Stardate 4738.3

The Klingon guards have boarded the *Enterprise.* Their doctors are obviously torn between moving Kalan and having him die, and allowing him to remain aboard an "enemy" vessel. The need for their commander seems to have won out. They have posted a close watch over him in the sick bay, much to Dr. McCoy's disgust. He is lodging a formal complaint over this invasion of his territory.

Kalan continues to heal rapidly. He will be able to return to the *Terror* shortly. But before then, we must conclude negotiations for peaceful occupation and joint cooperation on Alnath II.

Kirk walked into the sick bay flanked by Spock and Chekov. They passed the dour Klingon guards, who had their hands resting on their phasers, suspicious of anyone passing near their convalescing captain.

"I see you are doing much better, Captain Kalan," said Kirk. Both Spock and Chekov stood a half-pace behind him and to either side. Kirk disliked the need for such pomposity, but dealing with Kalan demanded it. If the Klingon even suspected weakness, he would not compromise on any point. Kirk had to maintain the façade of peaceful superiority, and having an "honor guard" attend him was part of the trappings.

"I will leave this pitiful ship soon, Kirk. My doctors

say they will be better able to serve me aboard the *Terror*."

"No doubt. But you must admit we have an extensive sick bay here. Nothing but top-of-the-line equipment and personnel to use it."

Kirk saw the grudging respect on Kalan's face. This was only one indication the Klingon commander had a way to go before complete recovery. If he had been totally fit, he'd have shielded that envy of the sophisticated medical equipment and hurled back a scathing insult. Kirk decided the time was ripe for pressing the negotiations.

"Since you will be returning to your own ship soon, let's complete our negotiations concerning Alnath II."

"There is nothing to negotiate. We demand mining rights to the topaline. *All* mining rights."

"Other mineral rights, too?" asked Spock mildly. "This is a virgin planet, for all intents and purposes. The prior race left it remarkably pristine, a variety of useful deposits under the surface."

"We don't need a geological survey, Vulcan. We know what is there and the Empire claims it."

"Do you mind if we continue to study the city? An archaeological study hardly impedes your own mining operation, if mining is your goal."

"A few bones and leftover cities don't impress us," Kalan sneered. "We need the topaline for our life-support systems." Kirk shrugged, as if the matter were closed. Kalan continued, "When I return to the *Terror*, I expect Lt. Kislath to accompany me."

"Kislath?" asked Kirk with mock surprise. "But that's out of the question. He had the temerity to attack a Federation vessel on a peaceful mission. Unless the Klingon Empire wishes to take the full blame for his acts, we must hold him as an individual criminal."

"He is scum," agreed Kalan, "but he is *our* scum. We will deal with him as we see fit. No weakling Federation ship filled with half-breeds and fools can mete out justice to one of our soldiers."

"You have little choice in the matter, Captain," pointed out Spock, his eyes flashing angrily. "Kislath fired on the *Enterprise*, he attempted to murder the captain, his actions are contralegal in many ways. We cannot allow him to return to his home planet light-years away. Justice must be served."

"It will be," said Kalan coldly. "Vulcan, you come close to realizing how we punish criminals. If it weren't for the cowardly streak running through you, you'd make a fine Klingon. When we punish, we *punish*. Kislath has committed crimes against the Empire. The other charges are ridiculous and trivial."

"Not trivial, Captain," said Kirk. "We're keeping Kislath. He'll be brought to trial at Starbase Sixteen when we return, and from the evidence of our recordings, he should be convicted. He'll be duly sentenced and probably spend the rest of his life on a prison asteroid."

"Prison asteroid? That's all? Weaklings! Kislath is a soldier of the Empire. Punish him properly. Don't put him away to molder like some animal. Give him a fitting death. Painful, yes, he should pay for his crimes, but put him to death. For honor's sake!"

Kirk suppressed a smile creeping onto his lips. This was the first time he had seen Kalan truly shocked. The facade of superiority had cracked, and now the Klingon reacted honestly. Kirk shook his head slowly, appraising the alien lying on the bed. The differences in their philosophies were almost insurmountable, but he had to not only see the universe through Kalan's eyes now, he had to be able to use that insight against the Klingon. Diplomacy, after all, was the art of doing and saying the nastiest things in the nicest possible way.

"We have our own code. For instance, stealing artifacts from an archaeological site before the scientists have examined them ranks as a high crime."

Chekov moved against Kirk's elbow. Kirk silenced the ensign with a quick hand gesture. Kalan's face paled slightly, another sign he was less than totally healed.

"What do you mean by that?"

"Threllvon-da tells me that artifacts were removed from the pyramid before our arrival. He claims that the Vulcans weren't responsible even though they entered the chamber before him."

"And what do these allegedly stolen artifacts look like?"

"Come, come, Kalan. We both know. The few baubles might not seem to be worth much, but to a scientist they are. For example, I find it difficult to believe they might be worth as much as mining concessions for topaline. Or the return of an officer suspected of high crimes and treason."

"You are blackmailing me, Kirk," said Kalan in a low voice. "Your own foolish laws cannot allow this, and my honor demands that I not give in."

"Nonsense, Kalan. How can I blackmail you—unless you are the one responsible for stealing those artifacts? Unless you have them aboard the *Terror?*"

"Perhaps the Klingon archaeologists were merely studying them," suggested Spock. "Such an exchange of knowledge might be considered valuable in diplomatic circles. A coup in the cause of interstellar peace and understanding."

"Yes, Mr. Spock, that's quite possible. But we know they would be more than willing to return all they've taken after the examination was over." Kirk studied Kalan's face as the Klingon commander fought with the dilemma facing him.

If Kirk had been a mind reader, he wouldn't have been better able to see the conflict. Kalan, on the one hand, wanted Kislath back. The former first officer had plotted mutiny, had tried to kill his commander, had disobeyed direct orders and, in some way Kirk didn't understand, was tied into the power structure back in the heart of the Klingon Empire. A triumph over Kislath gave a major political victory to Kalan.

But to get the miscreant back, Kalan had to admit stealing artifacts from the ebony pyramid. Whatever those artifacts were, they resided safely in the Klingon vessel. They were valuable in and of themselves. Their intrinsic worth paled next to admitting he had stolen the baubles. Kirk and Spock had given a slight opening that might be turned to benefit, if he played this hand to its logical conclusion.

"Yes," said Kalan slowly, "my scientists are examining the jewel taken from the pyramid. It appeared to be the only item worthy of our study, after a cursory examination of the pyramid's main chamber."

"Then you had no real intention of keeping this jewel?" said Kirk, learning for the first time what had been removed.

"Of course not. What use are pretty trinkets to a Klingon?" Pain etched Kalan's features; not the pain of physical discomfort, but the pain caused by yielding to beings he considered inferior. "I believe the jewel can be brought over at the same time Kislath is transferred back to the *Terror*."

"I see no problem with this. Do you, Mr. Spock?"

"None, Captain."

"See to it, then. And Dr. McCoy, is your patient fit enough to transport back to his ship?"

"He can transport into the heart of the sun for all I care."

"The feeling is mutual, butcher of men," snapped Kalan. McCoy bit back a retort as the Klingon gestured imperiously to his guards to wheel him from the room and to the transporter.

"Good riddance," the doctor said as Kirk left. The captain turned and smiled. He hurried down the hall to overtake the Klingon party. Ensign Chekov matched their pace a meter behind, keeping all of them under close surveillance.

In the transporter room, Spock already had brought in Kislath for the transfer. The Klingon stood rigidly, his eyes staring at a blank metal bulkhead. He gave no sign that he realized Kalan and the others were in the same room.

"The jewel, Kalan," said Kirk. "Then we can transfer the rest of the agreed upon merchandise." Kislath started at being called "merchandise," saw the lack of sympathy on any of the faces and only sneered. Under the mask of bravado was clearly fear of his punishment back aboard the *Terror*. To his credit, he said nothing.

Kalan pulled out a tiny communicator, flipped it open and spoke briskly into it. Closing the device, he told Kirk, "Your transporter chief has the coordinates locked in. Transport the gem now."

Lt. Kyle waited for Kirk's curt nod before moving the controls slowly. When they hit full transport stops, the column of coruscating energy formed and blinked out abruptly. In the center of the transporter disk lay a brilliant green jewel. For long seconds, Kirk stared at it in awe. It touched something deep inside him, made him want to laugh and cry and ... *achieve*.

"Dr. Threllvon-da will be most pleased with this addition to his report on the civilization once inhabiting Alnath II. I trust your scientists are finished with their investigations?"

"For some while," said Kalan, betraying a slight nervousness. "I have had it locked in my personal vault for safekeeping."

"Of course," said Kirk. "If you gentlemen care to beam back to your ship now, Lt. Kyle tells me he is ready for the transfer."

The Klingon guards helped Kalan to his feet. He winced in pain but didn't cry out. They supported him to one of the transporter cells, where he managed to stand unaided, though with great effort. Kislath marched onto another of the transporter disks, silent and withdrawn.

"May all our ventures end so successfully, Captain Kalan."

"May death come swiftly, Kirk."

The transporter energized, caught the Klingons and flung them across space back to their own ship. After the turbulence died down, there remained no hint that anyone had been in the transporter chamber. And for that, James T. Kirk was glad. It had been a long day.

"I don't want anyone approaching the stone, much less handling it," Kirk ordered. "Use anti-grav beams to move it around. That thing is potentially dangerous."

"Aye, aye, sir," said Chekov skeptically, moving around the shining gem, wondering if it might bite at any instant. "Where should it be stored? Vaults are not as plentiful on *Enterprise* as aboard Klingon ships."

Kirk smiled mirthlessly and said, "Get a rodinium box and place it inside. If you can find any material in engineering that's more dense, more obdurate, more refractory, use that. Ask Mr. Scott for his opinion on the matter, if he can spare the time away from his engines."

"Aye, aye, sir," said Chekov, going off to consult with Scotty.

"Might I inquire as to the purpose of the rodinium casing, Captain?" asked Spock. "The jewel is interesting from a crystallographic standpoint, but hardly requires shielding more in line with a matter-antimatter containment vessel."

"You're wrong about that, Spock. But tell me what your tricorder says about the jewel."

Spock raised one eyebrow. "A most fascinating crystal. The green tint, of course, is due to nickel. The matrix material is quasi-organic, neither living nor truly dead. That requires further study."

"It's alive?"

"Hardly, Captain, any more than any crystal is alive. Place it in a supersaturated solution of its constituent atoms and it will grow. But this specimen has certain additional qualities about it that remind me of a virus."

"A virus, Spock?" asked McCoy, coming into the room. "That thing's no virus. It's bigger'n a sheep's tonsils. We've never discovered a virus weighing more than five million daltons or bigger than six thousand angstroms."

"I said it had the qualities of a virus, Doctor, not the full structure or characteristics. For instance, it lives without having the self-contained mechanism of reproduction."

"It has to infect another cell to reproduce?"

"Unknown, Doctor. I am at a loss to say what cell could possibly contain a particle that large. Again, it has certain quasi-living elements about it while retaining many of the peculiar qualities of a crystal of orthorhombic structure, perhaps having symmetry elements of *Pmna* or *Pmm2*. Further investigation will resolve this."

"Spock, dammit, man, aren't you the least bit interested in what that thing *is?*" demanded McCoy.

"Indeed, Doctor, more so than you from all appearances."

"I'm not talking about what it's made from; I mean its importance."

"I haven't neglected that in my report, either."

"No more bickering, you two," said Kirk. "I need to know as much about that bauble as possible. Did you run an internal energy profile on the crystal, Spock?"

"Jim," said McCoy, horrified, "you're getting to be as bad as he is. Internal energy?" McCoy turned and stalked out, throwing up his hands in disgust.

"The doctor's emotional outburst is inexplicable," observed Spock.

"No, it isn't. But my theories can come later. Just continue holding on to your logic for a while longer." The frightened, pained look fleeing across Spock's face showed the intense struggle still raging inside him. Kirk guessed at the effort required to hold back that flood of very human emotion.

"The internal energy is off-scale," said Spock. "I have no indication of tricorder malfunction."

"Is the reading similar to the one first taken on Alnath II?"

Surprise etched the lines of Spock's face. He fought the emotional demands on his body again, slowly losing the battle. His jaws clenched and thick cords of tendon stood out on his throat.

"Yes, Captain. I remember what happened down there clearly. Candra told me about it. Candra did . . ." His voice trailed off and Spock got a dreamy look in his eyes. Then, as if a switch had been thrown, his far-off gaze hardened again—but didn't go all the way to machine as it had in the past. Kirk studied his first officer for a few seconds, then smiled.

"I think you're getting back to normal. Perhaps McCoy is, too. I despair of him operating using rusty jackknives and knitting needles, though I will miss his whiskey anesthetic."

"You know more of this affliction than you are telling, Captain," accused Spock, his voice quavering slightly.

"All in time, Spock. I take it that Mr. Chekov has the jewel safely locked away in its rodinium box. Order him to put it inside the heaviest force fields Scotty can conjure up. And then Threllvon-da, Avitts and McCoy meet me in the wardroom in one hour. Carry on, Spock."

"Thank you, Captain." Spock watched Kirk leave, whistling and a spring in his step that hadn't been there earlier. The Vulcan lowered his eyebrow and went to work. He had much to do and little time to accomplish it. Things were returning to normal.

"How're things in the sick bay, Bones?" Kirk asked as he seated himself at the table in the wardroom.

McCoy took his feet off the table and leaned forward. "Damnedest thing I ever saw. I jumped all over M'Benga and Nurse Chapel. I had them go over every single gadget in the place—and guess what they found?"

"All the instruments worked perfectly. Not a malfunction in the lot."

"You're telepathic. Some mutant gene give you precognition?" said McCoy in amazement. "That's exactly what happened. I tried out several of the computer-assisted devices myself, and they worked as well as if they were brand spanking new. I was in mortal fear all the while I operated on Kalan that those turncoat machines would give out on me, but they didn't. And now all of them are working."

Kirk nodded. Lt. Avitts and Spock entered, both looking vaguely uneasy.

"Be seated, please," Kirk said, motioning to a pair of seats next to him. "I wanted a few words with you before Dr. Threllvon-da beams up. Lt. Avitts, have you conferred with Mr. Spock on the nature of the crystal?"

He watched her reactions carefully. Her answer didn't matter to him, but the way she phrased it meant a great deal. The woman appeared as calm as she ever had been when Spock's name was mentioned. She turned slightly toward the science officer, a fleeting smile dancing on her lips, but that was the only response. She acted more like an officer aboard a starship than a lovesick teen-aged girl now.

"Yes, sir, but we have little to report without a full analysis of the jewel. As long as it's inside Class 7-E force shields, with six centimeters of rodinium box inside that, we have scant opportunity to study it."

"Are there any radiation cells available where you could open the box and examine it?"

"Captain Kirk, that crystal is not giving off any detrimental radiation," said the woman. "We've been over it with every possible radiation monitoring device. From cosmic rays through radio waves, there is nothing of a harmful nature."

"I know, but my order is that the rodinium box is never to be opened unless inside a radiation cell, using the most stringent precautions possible. Is that clear?"

"Yes, sir, but—"

"No buts, Lieutenant. I'm not a scientist as you are, but I have theories of my own concerning the crystal. I believe it is . . ." Kirk was interrupted by the blue-skinned Andorian scientist's arrival.

"There you are, Kirk. A major find in the city, yes, a major find. This is even more exciting than the rail transportation system we found that ran under the streets. This is the motive power for the piezoelectric walls in the city. Would you believe they used a thermal gradient device? As long as there is a heat difference between the city and the surface, electricity is supplied to the walls. Remarkable, isn't it? We can learn much from this city, Kirk."

"Uh, yes, Dr. Threllvon-da, I'm sure we can. But let's discuss a few other matters needing resolution."

"What can there be? An entire planet laden with mystery begs for my time. You've kept me from my equipment, Kirk, and that's criminal. But I will overlook it due to the nature of recent discoveries."

"That's kind of you, Doctor. I'm sure my superiors at Starbase will be pleased you aren't filing a negative report on the *Enterprise*'s conduct of the Klingon question."

"Klingons?" asked Threllvon-da, turning his broken ear stalk around for the first time. "What've they got to do with this? A nuisance, nothing more. Let them dig. Avitts, there, didn't she say all they wanted was to grub out topaline? Let them, as long as they don't use ultrasonics or explosives. Might hurt the ruins, you understand."

"We are working on a treaty with the Klingons that will explore such limitations on their activities. But I need to have a statement for the record concerning the pyramid and the chamber inside it."

"The pyramid?" he asked querulously. "That thing? Only the stepping-stone to the city. Nothing more."

"Yes, Doctor, I'm sure," said Kirk, exasperated. He took a deep breath and launched back into his request. "Please tell me all you can remember of the sequence of events immediately after you landed on Alnath II."

"I've done so," said Threllvon-da. "You forget too easily, Kirk. You'd never make a good archaeologist. No computers when you're out in the field. We have to keep track of millions of details in our heads. Seconds can mean a major discovery or finding rubble."

"The pyramid," prodded Kirk.

"We landed. The Vulcans and my crew. We began examining the perimeter of the pyramid to discern its nature and composition while the Vulcans went into the main chamber. They left, transported back up, and we never saw them again. On the heels of their departure came the Klingons. Brutish fellows, those Klingons. They bulled their way into the chamber, nosed around disturbing things, then left. When they returned, they brought huge diggers. Never went near the pyramid again because they were too busy trying to dig down through the vault of the city—*my* city. Did you know that Larldezz is going to propose to the Council that the city be named in my honor?" Threllvon-da sat down in the chair and beamed.

"A great honor, I'm sure," said Kirk dryly. "So the Klingons could have taken artifacts from the chamber, and you wouldn't have known?"

"I suppose," said Threllvon-da slowly. "We counted on the Vulcans to take holopix and make an inventory of all they found. With them dead, I know only what we found in the chamber later."

"What was the purpose of that altar at the end of the chamber?"

Threllvon-da shrugged impatiently. "Some religious observance was held in the room, I suspect. The empty holder in the center of the altar suggests a device the size of a large egg once rested there."

"Something this size?" asked Spock, flashing a picture of the jewel onto the computer screen.

"Could be. About the right size, if your computer scaling is accurate."

"It is, Doctor," said Spock, unruffled. Kirk smiled. Spock didn't get the least bit upset over questioning his competence now. A good sign, as was the way his first officer and Avitts sat side by side without visible discomfort.

"We have reason to believe the Klingons stole this from the chamber, due to its apparent worth."

"If it's an emerald, it might be worth something," admitted Threllvon-da, his gnarled fingers tapping restlessly on the table. "But as an artifact of this race, it's worth more. Knowledge is always worth more, always. But I can't be bothered with studying this now. The city is taking up more and more of my time. I must get back to it immediately. Are you going to require further expert advice, Kirk? You've held me back long enough. I want to devote my full attention to the find."

"I'll keep you posted, Doctor. Thank you for taking the time." Kirk spoke to an empty seat. Threllvon-da had flown from the room, intent on returning to the site about to be named in his honor.

"He worked like that the entire time I was on planet," said Avitts. "He's insatiable when it comes to work. The Klingons were only minor annoyances to him. Their digging bothered him the most because of the damage they might inadvertently cause."

"He hasn't changed much, has he?" asked Kirk.

"Changed from what, Jim?" asked McCoy. "He's still the most cantankerous, insulting, provincial—"

"Be careful, Doctor, or one might assume you were describing yourself," said Spock. "By your leave, Captain, I have matters to attend to."

"Dismissed, Spock. You, too, Lieutenant."

"They're probably going off to hold hands," McCoy said.

"Is that your best shot at him, Bones? No, I don't think they're going to do any such thing. While the *Enterprise* hasn't quite returned to its normal smoothly functioning self, it's a long way from the madhouse it became when we went into orbit around Alnath II."

"You sound sure of yourself," said McCoy suspiciously. "Have you isolated the force that's been making the crew so . . ."

"So cantankerous, insulting and provincial?" supplied Kirk. "I believe I have. Let's just wait and see if all's well aboard the *Enterprise* now, Bones."

The doctor shook his head, then left. Kirk sat for a moment, smiled and left the wardroom, too. The Klingons still presented a menace, though a minor one now. More of an annoyance, he told himself smugly. He felt too good about his ship, himself, his officers and crew, to worry about Klingons now. Whistling his jaunty tune, he entered the turbo-elevator and surged off for the bridge.

Candra Avitts hurried along the corridor, hardly noticing the people around her. Her mind was lost in the intricacies of the problem Spock had posed for her study. He had pronounced her weak in physics; she endured his tutoring, sure that she'd never be able to develop his instinctive grasp of the subject. Biochemistry was more to her liking.

She slammed into another woman coming around the bend in the corridor. They both gasped, took a backward step and spoke to apologize at the same time. And then both fell silent.

Lt. Avitts faced Nurse Chapel. The electric tension in the air between them mounted. It was as if two archenemies had met in the arena for the final duel.

"Lt. Avitts."

"Nurse Chapel."

They simply stood for several heartbeats, studying one

another and seeing what weaknesses might be exploited. The silence was broken by Lt. Avitts sighing and then laughing.

"This is ridiculous; you know that, don't you?" she asked.

"Why is it ridiculous?"

"We're fighting over something neither of us can ever have."

"It's not the first time in history. It won't be the last." Nurse Chapel locked eyes with Avitts, then smiled. Soon, she, too, laughed. "You're right. We've been behaving like schoolgirls with a mad, passionate crush on the handsomest boy in class. It's not that way at all, is it?"

"No, Christine, it isn't." Shyly, Avitts asked, "I may call you Christine, can't I?"

"Only if I can call you Candra. Look, isn't this a bit public? Let's go to my cabin. I've got some Denebian liqueur I smuggled aboard."

"The kind with the pepperminty taste?"

"None other than."

"I'll be happy to join you, Christine. I had some of that, but like a fool I traded it off for a chance to use the mass spectroscope in the chemistry lab. Spock wanted an analysis of some space debris we'd found—and he wanted it fast. My turn at the mass spec wasn't for another forty-eight hours, so I bribed the guy ahead of me and got the analysis done. Spock never knew what I gave up for him."

Christine Chapel stopped and said, "He'll never realize what either of us are giving up for him, will he?"

"No," sighed Avitts, "he won't. Perhaps that's what attracted me to him. His dedication. His brilliance. I don't know. It was a silly infatuation. I'm sorry we ever quarreled over it."

"If you have to quarrel over something, what better topic could it possibly be than Mr. Spock? Oh, Candra, you'll never know the hours I've spent thinking about him. Or maybe you do know. He's so distant, and yet I know that the human part of him needs loving, touching, the things his Vulcan self denies."

Avitts sat on the edge of the small hard bed in Nurse Chapel's quarters and sipped at the Denebian liqueur. "Umm, this *is* good. I'm sorry now I traded my liter for anything. Next time Spock wants something done by yesterday morning, I'm going to tell him it's not possible. Some things are just too good to pass up in life."

Christine Chapel felt hot tears coming to her eyes, but she held them back. "Yes, you're right. Some things are too good to miss. But we do anyway, don't we?"

"I tell you, Sulu, my fingers came this close to firing," Chekov declared, holding thumb and forefinger a millimeter apart. "I wanted to destroy the Klingon ship. Even though I knew my orders perfectly, I *wanted* to see them blown into millions of atoms."

"I know what you mean, Chekov," said the helmsman. "I had the conn when they fired on us. I remembered what you'd done and held off, but only barely. It's been so long since we had a good fight that I came close to disobeying the captain's orders, too. Strange. I'm not usually like that."

"No?" scoffed Chekov. "You enjoy a good fight like all of us. You said it. It has been a long time since the *Enterprise* engaged in a worthwhile space fight. Ah, to hear the phaser banks crackle and snap with teravolt discharges, to feel the shudder of the *Enterprise* as photon torpedoes launch—that is living."

"And dying, but I have the same feelings. Sometimes I wonder why we're trained to fight when we spend most of our time trying not to." Sulu idly checked his controls. They were locked for the orbit they now held. Unless Captain Kirk entered a course change, they would remain in this orbit shadowing the Klingon vessel, protecting the surface of Alnath with the hull of their own ship.

"It's easy to begin war but it's hard to end one," said Chekov. "I begin to understand some of the captain's problems. Hotheaded, I would have fired and created an instant war. Or maybe we would not be destroyed by the Klingons, and others would be embroiled in a war of our causing. Not a pleasant thought."

"It's easy to start a war, but hard to end one," mused Sulu. "You're right, Pavel. Umm, look sharp. The readout on circuit nine shows an overload. If we had to fire a photon torpedo, we might burn out a guidance circuit."

"Checking," said the ensign, turning his attention to his board. Soon the pair was engrossed in a mock battle problem, attempting to attain the maximum damage with the minimum expenditure of energy and materiel. With luck—and brains—they'd never have to put such knowledge to use.

"But is it worth it, lass?" asked Scott, as he peered into the bowels of the warp engine exciter. " 'Tis too much work for too little gain, as I see it."

"Aye, Commander Scott, you might be right," said Heather McConel, "but with so much work in the auxiliaries, shouldn't we try?"

"Not for only an extra percent of increased power. We've hit the diminishing returns stage," sighed the chief engineer. He stared at the computer controlling the warp engines. They had designed several devices capable of augmenting the power of those engines, usually at the expense of other ship's systems. Scotty shook his head, wondering how he could have ever pirated the autochef the way he had. The ship's nutrition officer still hadn't forgiven him for taking the controller. While the purple gruel had been nourishing, it wasn't appealing. Nor was the blue semiliquid compromise coming out after Scott had bollixed together a replacement for the autochef controller.

He sighed. It would have been so bonny to supplement the warp engine power by twenty percent or more. It seemed less likely now that they'd tried everything imaginable. Perhaps if he returned the autochef controller, he could inveigle the nutrition officer to program some haggis for the crew. That would set things right all around.

"Mr. Scott," said Heather hesitantly, brushing back her lustrous red hair with a strained hand, "would you think less of me if I suggested returning the laser I wheedled out of the metallurgy lab?"

"What? Oh, not at all, lass. But we need that laser to—"

"Please, Mr. Scott. It's just not working the way we'd intended. I think major breakthroughs will have to come from the scientists doing the basic research, not from the likes of us out among the stars a' tinkerin' with the precious engines."

"You might be right, but letting a paper-shuffler tell me what's good an' what's nae good for the *Enterprise*'s engines makes me fightin' mad." He stared over the equipment, trying to remember how much time they'd put in on constructing this plumber's nightmare. He chuckled. "But it hasna been a complete loss, now has it, lass?"

The twinkle in her eye told him that it hadn't.

"I'm off punishment duty in an hour, Mr. Scott," she said impishly. "If you're free, perhaps we can . . . discuss engineering."

"And other things?" he asked, smiling broadly.

"Like the bottle of Scotch you have—and other things," she agreed.

"Aye, but that bottle's almost empty. Only a wee bit left. But I have connections and might be able to find some spirits elsewhere."

"Don't worry, Mr. Scott," Heather told him. "I've got connections of my own. And the still's been working again for some time."

"Don't tell me about it!" he cautioned.

" 'Twas the gambling that did me in before. That's all open and aboveboard," she said. "The contra-regulation gambling is as honest as I can make it now, though the temptation's great to use just a wee electric field on the dice."

"What would that do?" asked Scott, in spite of himself.

"If I kinna use a laser on the roulette wheel, it occurred to me that a wee electric field might change the roll of the dice—if the spots were treated with a special paint I stumbled across that has decidedly electromagnetic properties. Just to change the tumble of those dice would . . ."

Chief engineer and assistant sat and discussed the possibilities inherent in this new gambling venture while sipping the alcohol distilled through the coils in back of the precision machine shop.

Chapter Eleven

Captain's Log: Stardate 4744.8

Tensions have eased considerably since the jewel from the pyramid was placed inside the rodinium box. The Klingons are amenable to negotiation for the mining concessions on Alnath II, the *Enterprise* functions at its normal high efficiency and another interstellar conflict has been averted. The only unexplained occurrence is the death of the Vulcans, and I believe I have an idea what happened. It will remain for a fully equipped science ship to test my theory, but they will know what to expect and can avoid the trap.

"You treat that thing as if it were an antimatter bomb, Jim," said McCoy, eyeing the precautions taken to insure that the jewel from the pyramid was shielded by both rodinium and radiation baffles.

"It's potentially worse, Bones. Mr. Spock, have you examined the pyramid?"

"Yes, Captain, and I am unable to discern what mechanism in the jewel's holder renders it harmless. It appears to be nothing more than a simple cup cut from rock but our knowledge of this planet and its prior inhabitants is still sketchy. They were obviously more advanced than even Threllvon-da believes."

Kirk nodded. He saw that Spock had worked through

the problem in his own logical way and had come to the same conclusions he had arrived at with more emotional reasoning. But it no longer mattered. They weren't threatened anymore by the massive, powerful Klingon dreadnought. As soon as Kalan had gotten back safely to the *Terror*, the tension between the Federation and the Empire ships had eased.

Kirk wished it could have vanished totally, but that wasn't the Klingon way. They were warlike and would continue to agitate. That was their life. Long years of diplomatic work were needed before the underlying causes of the friction between the cultures eased to the point where war became unthinkable. Kirk hoped he'd live to see that day. But now he had other, more immediate problems to deal with.

Like the jewel.

"Beam down, Spock. Get that thing back where it belongs. I want a security detachment to remain in and around the pyramid to prevent Threllvon-da and all his scientists from entering to examine the jewel."

"He won't like that, Jim," McCoy observed. "He's mighty touchy about your telling him what to do. Still blames you for not getting his precious equipment for him out of the *T'Pau*."

"I doubt he'll even notice. He's too busy rooting around in the city. You have your orders, Spock. Carry them out."

Spock, the densely swathed box with the jewel and five security men flickered out of existence in the *Enterprise*'s transporter to reappear on the surface of the planet below. The jewel returned home, where it belonged.

"We will destroy you, weakling!" shouted Kalan.

Kirk studied the swarthy face and decided that Kalan ranted only for effect. There was little left for them to disagree on. Still, diplomacy called for the Klingon—and him—to go through the motions and finally extract the promises both sides knew were forthcoming. Kirk both loved and hated the process. Unlike war, diplomacy was seldom straightforward, and the gains were often subtle, yet it was that very subtlety that intrigued him. That and the fact that the gains did not require death.

"Do you intend to attack, Kalan? If you do, the

topaline will be destroyed. You need the ore more than you need the battle."

Kalan subsided, glowering at Kirk.

"Further," Kirk went on, "there is no reason why both Federation and Empire can't share this planet. We have no desire to mine here. Our quest is for knowledge."

"Cowards," muttered Kalan.

"But we will fight if you try to prevent our scientists from exploring this planet's prior civilization and the ruins left behind. Do I make myself clear?"

"We have the mining rights, you dig for bones, is that it?"

"Essentially, Kalan."

"How do we insure that you won't try a backstabbing attack on our miners?"

"In the same way the Federation will guarantee the support and safety of our scientists. A squadron of ships in orbit will provide insurance that the other side will live up to the terms of this agreement."

"How many ships?"

"An equal number, with equal firepower. Also, both sides may maintain relay stations—any number—at the perimeter of the solar system to keep unimpaired contact with our home bases."

Kalan thought this over. Kirk didn't have to read his mind to know that Kalan mentally calculated the time of transit for an Empire dreadnought and then compared it with travel times for a similarly powerful Federation countermove. He smiled slightly, and Kirk knew the alien had arrived at a number satisfactory to the Empire. Kirk didn't worry about an armed takeover, however. This mental exercise on Kalan's part was simply second nature to the Klingon.

"Done," declared Kalan. "Our first load of ore will be lifted out of the gravity well in fifty hours. Do not attempt to stop it."

Kirk nodded assent. "That's why we've reached a mutually beneficial agreement, Captain Kalan. We know your intentions are peaceful."

Kirk had to laugh when the Klingon snarled and terminated the transmission. Seeing his momentary anger at being branded "peaceful" was payment enough for the hard time he had given the *Enterprise* and its crew, Kirk thought.

"Admiral Tackett will be pleased with *this* report," Kirk said smugly. "It's going to be the highest efficiency report we've ever turned in."

"I agree, Captain," said Spock. "It is surprising that the crew can change so quickly." He stared at the columns of figures showing the response times to various mock problems that had been presented—and met—by the crew. "No trace of the stone's influence remains."

Kirk stopped in front of the mess hall, wondering if he should really continue with the efficiency report now. He took a deep breath and went inside, expecting angry catcalls and outright fighting. He stopped dead in his tracks and surveyed the peaceful, even cheerful scene. The crew members inside joked and laughed, eating from plates laden with food that didn't even hint at being purple gruel.

"Mr. Scott fixed the autochef," supplied Spock.

Kirk sighed in relief. He moved through the rows of tables and saw that the appetizing food was well received by the crew.

"Let's check out engineering deck, Spock. I want to see what Scotty's done to the engines."

Everything in engineering proved shipshape. Kirk marveled at the transition from cluttered deck to the shining, spotless perfection he found now. All of Scotty's berserk electronic plumbing had been removed, with only a few black boxes attached in unfamiliar places.

"Chief McConel," asked Kirk, "what is the purpose of this device? I don't remember it being here on the last inspection."

"That, Captain, is the product of Commander Scott's experiments. It's a primary exciter for the warp engines."

"What does it do, Chief?"

"It gives a bonny ten percent more power."

"Ten percent? And the other devices?"

"They give another few percent, Cap'n Kirk," came Scott's voice. "Those are all that worked. The rest wasna good enough for the *Enterprise*."

"Excellent, Mr. Scott. You have things under control, I see," Kirk said. "Uh, where is the still?"

"Still, Cap'n? Why, that's nae according to regs."

"And gambling devices, Mr. Scott? You don't know anything about contra-regulation gambling devices, do you?"

"Captain!" protested Scott. "This is my engine room, nae a cheap gamblin' emporium!"

"I'm sure it's not cheap, Mr. Scott. Carry on."

As Kirk and Spock got outside, Kirk asked, "Is the gambling fair, Mr. Spock?"

"There seems to be a certain flouting of the laws of probability on the dice. However, no one has complained."

"Continue to observe, Mr. Spock, and if Chief McConel gets out of hand with her gadgets, let me know. Now, let's finish up this efficiency report and get it sent off to Starbase."

"All hands prepare to leave orbit," ordered Kirk, sitting and happily watching the bridge crew perform their job expertly. No one grumbled, no one hinted that they were better able to command and best of all, none was eager to fire the phaser banks in the direction of the Klingon ship.

Kirk glanced over his shoulder at the sound of the turbo-elevator doors opening. McCoy walked briskly to the command seat.

"What can I do for you, Bones?"

"Answer questions, dammit," flared the doctor. "I just finished the report Spock filed on Alnath and the stone and the deaths of the Vulcans, and I don't understand it."

"I'm not so sure I understand it myself," admitted Kirk. "That's what happens when you pioneer new planets. That stone left behind is easily the most valuable and complex device ever invented."

"Invented? But it's organic. Partly so, at any rate."

"Spock doesn't even pretend to understand it," said Kirk. "That stone was the basis of civilization on Alnath. They built it or grew it or whatever, then used it."

"How?"

"It's in the report, Doctor," came Spock's unruffled voice.

"All that mumbo jumbo doesn't mean much to me. Give it to an old country doctor in words of one syllable or less."

"That would be very difficult, Doctor, since monosyllabic—"

"Spock, desist," ordered Kirk. "The best we can make out is that the stone produces anything you mentally desire. The people creating the stone were so advanced they had no need for buildings or fields for crops, for anything that didn't aesthetically please them. That's why the planet is in virgin condition."

"The stone *produced* whatever they wanted? They just thought, say, 'I want a ham sandwich' and they got it?"

"Just like that, Bones. Or a house or anything. That's where *we* ran into problems. Not only didn't we know the stone's power or how to properly focus it, we haven't eliminated our most basic animal desires yet. Those came boiling to the surface."

"The Klingons mutinied because each wanted to be commander of that dreadnought. We didn't have problems like that. Scott wanted to super-tune the engines; Kyle wanted to become a great sculptor; you wanted to return to simpler things," Spock declared.

"I actually caused the medical equipment to malfunction because I distrusted it?" snorted McCoy. "Preposterous."

"But true, Doctor. Our minds apparently have not developed to the point where we could wish for material objects and have the stone furnish only them, unlike the prior civilization. We longed for less tangible items, lusts they had resolved in themselves."

"Like emotion, Spock?" said McCoy sharply. "You wanted to be human and—"

"And I also wanted to be fully Vulcan," finished Spock. "I was torn between two diametrically opposed desires. That posed problems now resolved."

"You went in the wrong direction," observed McCoy. "You should have stayed a human. Even with all the emotional storms, it's better."

"Doctor, I've been both human and Vulcan. I prefer the Vulcan, thank you."

"I suppose you're going to tell me that logic won out."

"Yes, Doctor, because logic did triumph in this instance. It is more logical to remain in control of all my faculties rather than allowing external forces to buffet me."

"Never mind, Spock. You've slipped back, but there're still some things I don't understand about all this."

"To be sure," said Spock dryly.

McCoy glared at him, saying, "What happened to the

Vulcans? I don't see any possible explanation. You can't say the stone did it."

"That's because you are too clouded by emotion, Doctor. The stone did 'kill' the Vulcans, though I hesitate to use that term. The stone gives whatever is desired most. It is our imprecise use of it that creates problems. Do you remember my encounter on Alnath with the tiny spot of light?"

"So?"

"That is what the Vulcans saw. The dot of light promised what all logical, non-emoting beings want: to become pure intellects freed from physical bodies."

"The Vulcans just discorporated?" asked McCoy, astonished. "Just like that?"

"They attained their fondest dreams, the logical conclusion to a physical existence. They passed to another, higher plane of existence, one allowing them to pursue their individual concerns with a pure intellect."

"No bodies to feel, to experience," mused McCoy.

"A pure intellect freed of the shackles of a vulnerable body, Doctor. The stone gave it to them because all were sufficiently advanced mentally."

"And with you, it just sent you seesawing back and forth between emotions and intellect?"

"Essentially correct."

"If that's all settled, gentlemen, let's leave this planet. There are other worlds to explore," said Kirk.

"Not so fast, Jim. You didn't seem to have any problems. I admit I went overboard distrusting machines, but you did everything just right."

"Not everything, Bones. It just worked out right for us."

"The Captain is being too modest," said Spock. "Captain Kirk, like myself, found himself torn between two extremes. However, he coped better. One part wanted to be the perfect soldier, to engage and defeat the Klingons. As this was clearly impossible due to the overwhelming supriority given them by their dreadnought, he chose the diplomatic side of his character. He negotiated a peace without recourse to becoming a soldier."

"That stone brought out the good in some of us," said McCoy. "It's not so evil."

"It's a tool, nothing more. How we use that tool is all that counts. The prior civilization might have followed the road taken by my Vulcan compatriots and become pure intelligences roaming the galaxy. They might have discarded the stone—and their planet—because they evolved into something we cannot begin to imagine. However it is, they were a mighty and advanced culture compared with us."

"That city alone shows that," said McCoy. He wrinkled his brow, then exclaimed, "The city! You said the stone provided them with all they needed. Why'd they build an underground city?"

"That, Bones," said Kirk, "is going to shake up Dr. Threllvon-da. Remember, the stone creates whatever you want most. Threllvon-da wanted to find a city exactly like that one more than anything else. His work is his life. He's absolutely single-minded. He, alone of all of us, was able to unconsciously use the stone to focus his thought into material objects."

"The city," said McCoy in a low voice. "That means . . ."

"That the city was not constructed by the original inhabitants of Alnath II," Kirk said. "I'm afraid that's so. Threllvon-da wanted the city; he got exactly what he pictured in his mind's eye."

"This'll kill him."

"In a manner of speaking, the original inhabitants did construct the city," Spock said. "Their tool—the stone—performed the task. But I would not worry about Threllvon-da. He will be disappointed, but this discovery promises to be more important than any number of abandoned cities. This is the first active, scientifically superior artifact ever discovered. *That* will create a fame for Threllvon-da far beyond his archaeological circles."

"It'll still be a blow."

"He'll recover, Bones, just as we've recovered from the stone's effects on us. All in all, everyone has benefited."

"I don't know about that," said McCoy. "Spock might have been better off with emotions. The way he is now—"

"Mr. Sulu," said Kirk, drowning out McCoy, "warp factor five back to Delta Canaris. I want to return to some peaceful mapping, for a change."

The *Enterprise* shivered powerfully and hurled itself out among the stars to continue the infinite task of exploring new worlds.

THE PANDORA PRINCIPLE

A Romulan Bird of Prey mysteriously drifts
over the neutral zone and into Federation
territory. Captain Kirk and the crew of the
Enterprise investigate, only to find the ship
dead in space. When Starfleet orders the
derelict ship to be brought to Earth for
examination, the Enterprise returns home with
perhaps her greatest prize.

But the Bird of Prey carries a dangerous cargo,
a deadly force that is soon unleashed in the
heart of the Federation. Suddenly, the only
hope for the Federation's survival lies buried in
the tortured memory of Commander Spock's
protégé, a cadet named Saavik. Together Spock
and Saavik must return to the nightmare world
of Saavik's birth — a planet called Hellguard, to
discover the secret behind the Romulans' most
deadly threat of all…

If you have difficulty obtaining any of the Titan range of books, you can order direct from Titan Books Mail Order, 71 New Oxford Street, London WC1A 1DG. Tel: (01) 497 2150.

Star Trek novels 1 – 31	£2.95 each
Next Generation novels 1 – 10	£2.95 each
Star Trek novels *32* onwards	£2.99 each
Next Generation novels 11 onwards	£2.99 each
Star Trek Giant novels 2 – 5	£3.95 each
Star Trek Giant novels 6 onwards	£3.99 each
Next Generation Giant novels	£3.99 each
The *Star Trek* Compendium	£8.95
Mr Scott's Guide to the Enterprise	£6.95
The *Star Trek* Interview Book	£5.95
Worlds of the Federation	£8.95
Captain's Log	£5.99

For postage & packing: on orders up to £5 add £1.20; orders up to £10 add £2.00; orders up to £15 add £2.50; orders up to £20 add £2.70; orders over £20 add £3.70. Make cheques or postal orders payable to Titan Books. NB. UK customers only.

While every effort is made to keep prices steady, Titan Books reserves the right to change cover prices at short notice from those listed here.